Break/
Interrupt

The Synthetic Albatross
Series
Book Four

I0602147

Break/Interrupt
AdventureWorldsPress.com

First Printing. April 2021

Published By
Adventure Worlds Press
Windsor Ontario

Printed in Canada.

ISBN 978-1-7776616-0-1 (paperback)

Cover by Glen Hawkes
Author Photo by Khoa Nguyen

Break/
Interrupt

Ben Van Dongen

FOR MY FRIENDS
Who sat through a lot
of talk before I
actually wrote a book

ONE

It Started
With A Whimper

Spectators jostled around the table at the back of the bar. The smell of stale beer and sweat was mixed with an overly sweet grape fog expelled like smoke from a factory by one of the patrons. Ric waved the haze away as it settled on the game field, highlighting the display projected over the table. He clenched his teeth as the patrons pushed in closer. Staring at his competitor, he ignored the rapid flashing as the virtual battlefield cycled through random layouts. The VR Enclave Maze, once the definitive challenge for hackers, had become the domain of artificial intelligence.

The crowd yelled over each other, cheering for their chosen competitor and placing bets.

Ric half-smiled and leaned forward into the projection. "Hey. What's your name?"

The woman across from him sneered. Her teeth

sparkled as light reflected off the gems set in them. She wore dirty and tattered clothes the same colour as her tangled mane of unnaturally bright red hair.

He cupped his mouth to yell over the din. "Your name?"

"You'll learn about it when I'm famous."

Chuckling, he sat back. "Whatever you say." He had only met a few people who lived in the Wall, a nearby structure that cut through the city. Many of them were savage, like her.

The bartender placed a rock glass filled with pale yellow liquor in front of Ric. "Here you go, sport. No causing a ruckus like last time." His t-shirt had slipped up and showed a sliver of his massive beer belly. With a stained apron around his waist, the section of flesh looked like a fish mouth.

"I'm not in charge of how other people act, Tony." Ric looked up at the man. "This the real stuff?"

Tony wiped his hands on the apron. "Real as we get here."

Ric brought the glass to his nose and sniffed. He struggled to discern the fragrance of the liquid through the overwhelming smell of smoke and body odour, but there was a hint of woodiness in the liquor.

"It's made by real Mexicans, but they live somewhere north of the Wall." Tony bobbed his head in the direction of a series of old buildings that over the years had been connected together by the residents and turned into a barricade that dissected the megalopolis. The Eastern Urban Sprawl, an amalgamation of most of the eastern seaboard, was the largest city in North America, even when cut nearly in two.

Ric had forgotten the real name of the bar and called it The Fish Market like everyone else. It sat in the shadow of the dreaded Wall. Rumors of monsters in the underground maze kept kids out of the lawless place and, as Ric remembered from his own youth, gave them nightmares. Surrounded by the Wall on one side and giant street-straddling skyscrapers everywhere else, the bar remained in deep shadows most of the day.

Taking a sip of the locally-made tequila, Ric shuddered. "It's smooth." He coughed as he set it down. "It's a wonder no corporation has snapped this place up yet."

"Suits me just fine." Tony threw a towel over his shoulder and pushed through the crowd, waddling back to the bar.

"Hey!" The woman sitting across from Ric slapped a hand down. A splash of his drink sloshed out of the glass. "We doing this, or are you scared?" Pulling a wire from her forearm, she plugged it into a jack built into the side of the table.

Ric brushed back his bangs. He was overdue for a haircut and they kept falling in his face. "Okay, but don't get mad at me when my AI beats yours." He fished out his own cable from under his long-sleeve t-shirt. As soon as he was connected, a flood of information streamed through the wires built into his left arm to the core, a compute-unit the size of a deck of cards implanted behind his collarbone, and on its way to the main implant behind his left ear. The implant was a dense circuit smaller than a grain of rice that connected to the internet, cellular signals, and his private network. It projected a screen directly to the optic nerve, making it seem like it was floating out in front of his eye.

With the technology embedded around his body, he was able to house the artificial intelligence he'd been developing for over seven years. Together, they were contracted by companies to track down and clean infiltrations by outside hackers, competitors, and rogue AI.

Hunt, his AI, reached down the cable, through the interface, and into the table. "How long should I let it go on?" He giggled.

Ric could hear Hunt through the implant behind his ear, but the AI only spoke to him. His arm felt warm where the information flowed through the wires in his skin. He glanced down at the part of the table not taken up by the playing field and projected

4

a keyboard onto its surface. *Let's not get ahead of ourselves*, he typed.

It was easier to talk to Hunt verbally, but surrounded by people and his opponent, he kept it private. He even used an unusual layout for the keys. He was good enough to tell what people were typing by their button presses, real or VR, and there were people and AI way better than he was. *We don't know what kind of AI this woman has.*

"I'm the only hunter/cleaner we've seen so far. These battles are boring if I don't make it interesting."

I'm sorry they're not exciting for you, but we can use the street-cred. The notoriety from these back-alley matches helps us get clients. Ric masked his trepidation with a wink at the woman. She snarled like an animal and bared her shiny teeth. *You're old for an AI, but you're still a kid. Don't let a winning streak go to your head.*

"I don't have a head." Hunt chuckled.

I'm not debating metaphors with you again. You know what I mean. Ric remembered the first match he'd lost. It was the first AI he'd faced. The early model designed for traffic flow management had mopped the floor with him, which spurred him to create Hunt. It was at a nicer bar, but everything else about the match was the same. Except for his manic opponent.

"Ready or not, here we come!" the woman yelled. The lights around the table dimmed and the play-field glowed brighter as the woman initiated the match.

The multi-level sprawl of twisting tunnels looked like a plate of glowing red spaghetti stuffed into a glass box, but all the turns were at right angles. The woman's AI was as aggressive as she was. She, Ric assumed the AI was female as they usually chose the gender of their creators, charged forward, burning the tunnels behind her as she went. The red tunnels were scorched black, closed off to further travel. The crowd fell silent. There was a moment where it felt like the only thing moving in the bar was the woman's artificial intelligence sprinting through the maze.

One of the observers cheered and the space around the table exploded into chaos of noise and light. Ric watched Hunt, stationary at his starting point, letting his opponent dominate the match.

TWO
And Ended
With A Bang

Hey, Hunt. The match started. Ric typed the words in a hurry. Over the shouts, cheers, and jeers, he caught a distinct trend of bets leaving his side and favouring the challenger.

Hunt!

The AI didn't respond. Ric closed his left eye to better focus on the projected screen. He started a rushed version of his diagnostic program and reached for the manual joystick control built under his side of the table. Giving the stick a test wiggle, the only action in the play-field that changed was the opposing AI claiming a greater percentage of the maze. Gritting his teeth, he grabbed the jack coming out of his forearm and tensed, ready to pull it and disconnect Hunt.

"Not yet," Hunt said.

There you are. What's going on?

"You want to get noticed, right?"

Ric could imagine the AI smiling. Hunt didn't have a face, but Ric always pictured his brother's smirk when the AI pulled a risky stunt. *I want to win, especially against a barbarian from the Wall.*

"Just wait." The free space in the maze shrank as the woman's AI sped through it, eliminating the routes she didn't take.

Ric checked the display in the corner of his vision. Her side had claimed forty-five percent of the field. Someone in the audience bumped the table and spilled Ric's drink. The almost-tequila dripped off the edge and into his lap. Sneering, he swiped his hand, wiping away the liquid and knocking the glass into the crowd and eventually to the floor. "Come on, Hunt. Stop fooling around!" Ric yelled out loud.

When the count reached forty-seven percent, Hunt burned two tunnels. The virtual fire was so fast that it was hard to follow by eye. The laser-light went out, twisting across the maze. Ric tried to follow where the tunnels went, but lost track almost immediately in the complex labyrinth.

At forty-nine percent, Hunt pounced. He streaked across the field in a flash and cornered the woman's AI just as the tunnels he'd burned and the ones she scorched behind her, cut off any chance of escape. The match was over. Hunt had trapped his opponent in three moves.

The bar fell silent as everyone, including Ric, tried to catch up with what happened. The play-field flashed in multiple colours. The areas that had been burnt were still black, but the untouched fifty-ish percent glowed green and Hunt's path showed up in yellow. Above the maze, floating block letters rotated on the opposing ends of the field. Ric smiled at a spinning and tumbling 'WINNER' in front of him.

The woman shot to her feet and kicked the table. It was heavy with the game board built into it, but it still slid into Ric and pushed him back.

"Hunt." He stood, his expression stony, glaring at her.

"Say the word and I'll—" the AI started to say.

A meaty hand forced Ric down into his chair. The bouncer, a woman who claimed to have been part of a Corporate hit squad in her youth, squeezed his shoulder and slowly scanned the crowd with un-blinking eyes. Like the bar, Ric had once known her real name, but the nickname, Auntie Crush, had permanently taken that spot in his memory.

He winced under her grip. The audience found other things to occupy their attention and dispersed.

The defeated woman in red stepped onto her chair and roared, bashing her chest with a fist. She dove towards Ric, but Auntie caught her in midair and carried her towards the door. The woman, kicking, punching, and biting the much larger bouncer, was still plugged into the table and a cry of real pain broke through her snarling as it pulled taut before reluctantly disconnecting.

Ric watched it drag across the floor as she was carried out. He stood and rotated his shoulder to make sure it wasn't broken. In the scattered crowd, he spotted the greasy bookie collecting credits from the losers. The downtrodden patrons tapped their wrists or cards against his elbow. The bookie had once told him that he chose to have his chip implanted into his elbow to deter criminals from chopping off his hand to steal his money.

Shaking his head, Ric unplugged and sauntered to the bar. "Tony, some jerk spilled my drink." He gestured to his pants.

"You sure you didn't piss yourself when that woman nearly ran away with the match?" The bartender was busy pulling glasses from a tiny-rotating dishwasher.

"I almost did." Ric looked up, not towards anything physical, but it was where he visualized Hunt, floating above him in the ether. "Someone wanted to show off and didn't bother to tell me."

A fly buzzed around his head and then up to the ceiling. The slowly spinning fan forced it back down where it joined others flitting around a garbage can in spirals. The front door slammed shut and he turned to see Auntie take up her post. She half-sat on a high stool next to a weapons scanner.

With Auntie back on her perch, the regular din of the bar swelled back to life. Ric leaned closer to Tony who had finished putting the glasses away and was back to taking orders.

"I think I deserve to have my drink replaced." Grabbing a nearby stool, he pulled it under him.

"Should have had that woman replace it for you before Auntie threw her out." The bartender pulled a bottle of premixed something from a fridge by his knees and added it to a tall glass of vodka. The liquor was from a bottle of an expensive imported brand, but Ric knew it was really filled with more local hooch.

"She wasn't the one who knocked it over."

"Bother the person who did. I have a business to run." Tony slid the drink in front of the patron who'd ordered it and moved on to the next. "Come to think of it, I should charge you for that glass you broke."

When Tony turned to grab a new bottle from the shelf behind him, Ric slipped off the stool and pushed his way towards the back of the room.

"Hey," Hunt said in his ear. "Want me to connect with the security system and scrub through the video feed to see who did spill your drink?"

Ric tapped on his thigh, pressing virtual keys. *No. Stop snooping on people. It's a bad habit.*

"I'm just trying to help."

I know, but you have to stay out of private networks unless we're on a job—

"Or unless you order me to, right?"

Ric pictured his brother with his eyebrow raised and head tipped to the side. *Do as I say, not as I do.*

"Fine. It just gets boring seeing everything from your implant. You get so little information that way."

Finding an empty cocktail table, Ric touched the surface to make sure it wasn't wet or sticky. When his hand came back dry, he leaned on it and scanned the crowd for the bookie. *Why don't you work on some of the puzzles I made for you?*

Hunt sighed. The AI didn't breathe, but he had a habit of mimicking human mannerisms. Sighing, huffing, and whistles were his latest obsession. "All done. I wish we had another protection job. It's fun to sweep big corporate systems looking for weaknesses and setting traps for infiltrators."

Me too. If we want more of those jobs we need to build our reputation. Ric picked at his sleeve. *Tomorrow we have the Mahoney Semiconductor gig. You could start checking out their network.* He tapped a finger against the tabletop. *Public only. Don't go hacking into the servers of a client.*

"Uh. What if I—sort of—already did a sweep of their servers?"

Ric clenched his teeth. "Damn it, Hunt." The words slipped out. He glanced at the nearby tables, but no-one seemed to be paying any attention to him. *We've talked about this.*

"I know but I just sent a test probe and it went through. While I pulled it back I just happened to see some of their encrypted data."

Ric imagined his brother shrugging. *When did you do it?*

"Just now. After the match."

While I was talking to Tony at the bar? Ric shook his head. *I'm not condoning what you did, but since you already took a look, what's their issue?*

"Oh!" Hunt's virtual voice slipped up an octave. When he was excited, he acted and sounded more childlike. "I haven't gone through all the data, but they have a serious infestation. There are at least a hundred rogue AI infiltrating their network."

They didn't see you, did they?

"I can't be sure, but I doubt it. They were pretty low quality and really focused on burrowing deeper into the system."

Ric spotted the bookie by the game-table and waved the greasy man over. *There's a job for you. Analyze what you saw of the rogues, try to figure out what they're looking for, and make a plan to get rid of them for tomorrow. The faster we fix their problem, the better we'll look.*

The bookie stopped out of arm's reach from the table. He glanced behind him every few seconds, his greasy hair following the motions at a slight lag, exposing its weight. He wore a long coat, even though it was too warm in the bar. "What do you want?" The man scratched at a red patch on his exposed neck. "You didn't make a bet, so I don't owe you anything." The man's red eyes darted back and forth, settling on Ric for brief moments.

Hunt. Get rid of the encrypted data you took. Accidental or not, if anyone finds out, we're in trouble. Ric forced a smile to the bookie. "Hey. I don't remember your name."

"Good." The man blinked erratically. "I don't give it out for a reason."

"That's fine." Ric let the smile drop and brushed back his bangs. He resisted the urge to scratch his own neck, seeing the marks the bookie had left with his jagged nails. "I know you don't owe me anything, but you made a bundle off that performance. The least you could do is buy me a drink."

The bookie recoiled. "I can't set that precedent." He took another step away.

"Come on, man. Some jerk spilled mine during the match."

"Sounds like that guy owes you a drink. Not my problem."

Hunt whispered, even though no one else could hear him. "That guy has an infection around the chip in his elbow. That red around his neck shows how far it spread."

Screw him. He made probably a thousand credits on our match and won't even cop for a drink?

"But he's really sick. Unchecked he could die from an infection like that."

Ric jammed his tongue into the roof of his mouth.

The bookie looked behind him even more frantically. "Wha—what are you staring at? You're freaking me out."

With a huff, Ric gestured to the man's neck. "That rash isn't a rash. It's an infection. You should go to the clinic—"

"Right now!" Hunt said.

"As soon as you can. You could die."

"You threatening me!" The bookie flung himself backwards, colliding with a group huddling two deep around one of the cocktail tables. They pushed him back and the bookie fell at Ric's feet.

"I'm trying to help you out, you stingy idiot. If that infection reaches your heart, you'll die."

The bookie reached out his hand but Ric didn't help him up. "For real?"

Ric shrugged. "Believe me or don't, it's not my problem." Leaving the man struggling to get to his feet, he went back to the bar to order the cheapest drink on the menu.

Break/Interrupt

THREE

Brief Morning

Sunlight shone in Ric's face. Starting over a hundred and fifty thousand kilometres away, the rays missed the Corporate space stations, the growing cloud of satellites, gigantic skyscrapers, old buildings, tables, and chairs to reach him. He grunted and rolled onto his side. The sour smell of old beer and dirty shoes jolted him into a sitting position.

A long, slow rumble in his stomach gathered at his esophagus and worked its way out as a burp that he failed to cover under his hand. The display in his left eye showed him it was nine in the morning, within the small window of time where sunlight reached The Fish Market. A few other regulars were passed out farther back, away from the dirty windows. Ric was almost directly under the filthy panes, probably tossed there by Auntie Crush the night before when he'd had one too many and fell asleep at the bar.

Like many people scraping by, he lived in a tiny room just big enough for him to lie down. South of the Wall was more densely packed than the North, and most of the old apartment buildings had been converted years earlier.

Sleeping on a dirty bar floor was only slightly worse than going home, so it was a tossup each night where he would end up. The sunlight streaming through the window flickered as the mass of people constantly milling along the streets in the megalopolis passed the tavern.

"You're up!" Hunt said. "I was going to wake you if you didn't get up soon. We need to get ready for the Mahoney job." The AI's voice was as excited as a child on his first day of school. "Also, I picked up a familiar signal in the area."

Ric got to his feet and walked to the end of the long bar. The stools were up on top of it, but the floor was sticky. Once behind the counter, he poured himself a glass of water and fumbled with the coffee maker. "Damn it, Tony. Get a normal drip machine," he mumbled.

"I can walk you through it."

Shaking his head, Ric grabbed the bar to keep steady. "No. Tell me what you mean by familiar signal? Were you breaking into the city network again?"

"Just the local traffic and closed-circuit stuff.

Nothing deep enough to trigger security."

Rick brushed back his bangs. "How many times do I have to tell you not to do that, Hunt?"

There was creaking as Tony tromped down the stairs leading up from behind the bar. He wore a robe over a not-so-white t-shirt, the belt tied under his stomach. Ric saw his gut before anything else.

"Probably as many times as I've told you to not go behind my bar, Ric." Tony stopped at the last step and crossed his arms.

Ric put up a hand as he slunk past the man. "I didn't want to wake you up." Once safely out of reach, he covered one of his eyes, the hangover taking hold. "By the way, Tony. You got some pain meds you can spare?"

The bartender finished setting the coffee to brew. "You got enough to pay for this coffee?"

"I can." He stepped farther back, closed eyes facing the dirty floor. "Yeah, I can scrape that and my tab after today's job."

"And what's that one again?" Tony stretched over the bar, his gut limiting his reach. With a huff, he half-beached himself and dropped a couple of the stools back in place. "Take care of that, will ya?"

Ric took all the stools off the bar and started on the nearby tables. "It's a cleaner job at Mahoney Semiconductor. Big bucks. Almost enough to start looking for a new apartment."

Tony poured two cups of coffee and gestured to the one he left on the bar. "Who owns them now?"

"Like, what Corporate conglomeration?" Ric sat and picked up the cup. He smelled the bitter dark liquid and touched the warm mug to his face. "I think it's Amcoral?"

"That's a good gig. Real big time." Tony raised his own mug in acknowledgement. "Before you go looking for new digs you pay off your tab." The man pulled a packet out of the deep side pocket on the robe and flicked it to Ric.

The foil pouch hit him in the face and dropped next to his mug. "Tony, you're a true gentleman." Ric ripped open the single serving medication and poured the two pills into his mouth—washing them down with a sip of hot coffee.

"This your glass of water here?"

"I mean." Ric craned his neck to look, not trying too hard. "Which one?"

Tony shoved a sausage link finger in Ric's face. "Tab paid in full by the end of the week."

Ric shrugged. "Come on." He gestured to the people still snoozing in the back. "There are people with a way worse tab than me."

"And they take fewer liberties."

The door swung open, briefly letting in a flood of sunlight. Ric squinted and brought up his arm to cover his eyes. "Who the hell is that at this time of the day?"

"That's who I was trying to warn you about," Hunt said. "It's Chloe!"

Break/Interrupt

FOUR
Percentages

Ric could hear a slight whir of robotic components as the tall woman sauntered over to them. She wore a tight, cropped jacket with big shoulder pads over a flowing, sheer blouse. Her white leggings were see-through up to the tops of her thighs showing the large sections of metal augmentations surrounded by veins of skin the colour of caramel. Above that, her pants checkered into opaque black. She held her tiny nose in the air on her way to the stool next to him.

"I thought I'd find you here." She took off a pair of sunglasses that covered a third of her face. Her eyes, both implants, flashed as they adjusted to the light. The irises slowly changed from bright blue to purple as they focused on him. "That might even be the same stool."

Ric smiled too widely. "Been a while."

"No need for bitter tears my sweet boy." Chloe perched on the stool and crossed her legs. A twitch starting at her toes climbed up her leg and to her shoulder. She clenched her hand, causing more faint whirring sounds. "You need a haircut."

Brushing back his bangs, Ric picked up his mug and leisurely drank. He ignored the tremors in her inorganic parts. "What brings you back to this little corner of the planet? Feeling nostalgic?"

"I knew you'd be desperate and floundering without me and while I'm utterly occupied with my career, I felt like I should show some pity on the man who once promised to do anything for me." Chloe tucked her hands under her arms, hiding the increasingly obvious shaking. Her mouth was tight, but she managed her own smile.

"I appreciate your concern, Chloe, but there really was no need to worry." Ric glanced behind him at the bulk of the grubby tavern. "My reputation is growing, I have a few high-profile jobs lined up, and my winning streak with the VR Enclave Maze is record worthy."

"That's so cute. You're still playing that little game." Chloe covered her mouth with the tips of her fingers until they started to shake. Then shoved them back, pinned between her arm and side.

"You used to like watching me play." Ric focused on his mug. He drained the coffee, but kept his grip on the handle.

"I was a kid back then."

Ric huffed. "Well, this has been nice. Thanks for visiting, Chloe. Have fun modeling or whatever it is you do up on those space stations to keep the managers entertained."

Tony, busy weighing bottles, put one down hard.

"Fine." Ric glared at Chloe over his shoulder. "That was unkind, but you came here to see me."

Chloe looked at her knees. "I'm a little embarrassed, okay?"

Ric stood. "Alright. What can I do for you?"

Uncrossing her legs, Chloe held her hands out to him. They shook, as if she were shivering in the cold.

The longer Ric watched her, the more he noticed tics and twitches all over her body. "How long?" He grabbed her hands and leaned in to get a closer look.

She flinched at his touch. "I noticed last summer and it's been getting worse ever since."

"This is pretty bad, Chloe. How have you kept it under wraps?"

"It isn't normally this pronounced." She cleared her throat. "It's worse when I'm nervous. Which makes me more nervous, which makes it worse." Frowning, she glanced at him. "It's stupid."

Ric let her hands go. "You have more implants since I saw you last."

"Yeah. So?"

"How many?" He raised an eyebrow. "What percentage?"

Crossing her arms again, she nodded at his stool. He sat.

"Fifty-three."

Ric nearly fell off the stool. "Fifty-three? No wonder you're shaking like that."

Her jaw tight, she looked away. "It's not like that."

"Honey. The last time I saw you, you were less than thirty percent." Ric's leg bounced. "That's a hell of a jump in, what, two years? You have rejection sickness."

Chloe slapped the bar. "Bullshit, Ulrich. There's no such thing. I've met girls up there who are at sixty and they're fine! Besides." Grabbing his arm, she pulled back his sleeve. "You're one to talk."

"Yeah. I've got implants. Do you want to know my percentage?" He glared up at her. "Six. I am six percent cyborg by mass and four by volume." He pulled his sleeve back down. "I'm going to assume that after your first operation you've been getting your implants up on those Corporate space stations."

She opened her mouth but he put up a finger to stop her and she nodded.

"I know the first one was fine because I scanned you myself. I can't imagine the stuff you get up there," he pointed to the ceiling, "is anything less than top of the line. That means it's not hardware or software and you're too smart to miss maintenance or updates. It's the shakes and the most likely cause is rejection sickness. That's a lot of stress on a nervous system."

Chloe shook her head. "Rejection sickness is a myth spread by paranoid pure-human nut-jobs."

"I've seen it before." Ric furrowed his brow. "It's getting more common down here. I've looked into it, read the data."

"Oh, right." She rolled her eyes. "Because you don't go to the darkest, dankest places on the web."

"Chloe. You're a foot taller than me now." Ric held his hands up to measure their height difference.

"I've always been taller than you."

He let his arms drop to his sides. "Fine. I'm just trying to help. I can do a scan, see if there's anything in the code or," he shook his head. "I know a little about interfacing between synthetic and organic tissue."

Chloe shuddered, more obviously than the tremors plaguing her body, and sniffed. "I'm scared, Ric. I don't want to hear nonsense about made-up disorders."

"Okay. I'll let it drop." He shrugged. "Come over here so I can do a scan."

After a moment, she wiped her eyes and faced

him. "Thank you."

"Right." Ric looked up, where he imagined Hunt always hovering above him. "Hunt, I take it you've been listening?"

"You got it. I'll jump over and see what's there," the AI said in his ear.

"Whoa!" Chloe straightened. "You never said anything about that AI of yours doing the scan."

Ric smirked. "Really? He can do a more thorough job in a fraction of the time. If you want me to do it, we'll have to book a couple of weeks and get our hands on some hard to come-by equipment." He brushed back his hair. "On Earth, anyway."

Chloe grimaced. "You're sure it's okay. He's not going to monkey around in there?"

"You haven't seen him in years. AIs grow up very differently than people. He's more mature than some adults I know."

"That's right! You're safe in my hands," Hunt said. Ric could hear him, but the AI was addressing Chloe, so he figured Hunt was talking in both of their implants. "Not only am I restricted by the Cardinal Tenets of AI regulation in my base code, but Ric taught me not to mess with humans. It's part of my original protocols and it's been reinforced over years of his guidance."

Ric turned to Tony, who was done with the bottles and had moved on to cutting garnishes. "Can I get another cup when you got a chance? Chloe, you want one?" He glanced at the woman, but her eyes were closed. "Two, please, Tony."

The bartender put down the knife and meandered to the coffee pot, wiping his hands on the towel tucked into his apron.

"We do our best, right, Hunt?"

Chloe furrowed her brow, her eyes still shut. "You two have an interesting relationship."

Hunt chuckled. "He's the best friend-father an AI could ask for."

"Friend-father?" Chloe peered at Ric with one open eye.

He focused on Tony filling his mug. "Yeah. It's—Hunt thinks it's funny that I sort of raised him, but we're kind of friends. It's weird."

"It's great!" Hunt said. "I'm about a quarter of the way through this. Nothing so far. Just a few drivers that could stand to be updated."

"That's not out of the ordinary." Ric felt the compute-unit under his collarbone vibrate as Hunt pushed its CPU. The spot twinged a little like a sore muscle. He considered an upgrade if there was enough money left over after paying his tab.

Tony placed a mug in front of Chloe and pulled two little bowls from under the counter. One was filled with sugar and sweetener packages and the other with little cups of cream. "It's on him, sweetie."

Chloe opened a cream and poured it into the steaming mug. "Thank you, Tony. It's nice to see you." She stirred her coffee, the spoon clanking against the sides of the mug. "Oh. I meant to ask you two. Did either of you hear about the ship that flew overhead yesterday?"

"Overhead?" Ric perked up. "Like from the Wall?"

She shook her head. "To it, from one of the orbiting space stations."

He took a sip. "It must have been Telbak. They have a majority stake in the Wall, so any job there would have to go through them. Not that there is anything worth a Corporate mission in that cesspit."

Chloe's hands shook as she brought the drink to her lips. She took a hurried sip. "Hey. How's your brother been? He joined up with Telbak, didn't he?"

Ric ran his tongue along his top row of teeth. "It was Telbak, yeah, but we haven't really talked since he left."

"No?"

Picking up his mug, Ric grimaced at it and placed it back down. "Our goodbye wasn't very brotherly. He was so desperate to get off this planet and I didn't realize how much he really did for me." Ric sensed the implant in his shoulder again. He pressed hard, feeling the corner of the compute-unit. "He was against me getting the implants, never trusted them and," Ric cleared his throat. "I wasn't very pleasant when he told me he was joining a Corporate taskforce."

She touched his arm briefly and pulled her hand back as if his skin had scalded her. As if the impulse took over before she could stop herself. "I know what being willing to do anything to leave is like. I'm sorry it turned out that way. You two were really close."

He shrugged. "Can't do much about it now. About a year ago, around his birthday, I tried to contact him through the Telbak personnel listings." He shook his head.

"I don't think he works for them anymore. I've been spending a lot of time on the Telbak station recently and he's been mentioned, but I haven't seen him. One woman," Chloe laughed. "She's a real odd one. I've heard her tell a story or two about him."

Ric felt a smile tug at the corner of his mouth. "I'm not surprised he left an impression. I hope he's okay." He huffed. "I have a question for you."

"Okay." Her mouth tightened.

"It's—just bear with me." Rocking, he slid his stool closer to her. "Have you heard anything about a secret, unauthorized merger of some of the smaller companies? Something called the Consortium."

Chloe crossed her arms. "More dark-web conspiracies?"

"Just rumors. A few people at some of the jobs I did for smaller subsidiaries told me some stuff, but I haven't found anything concrete."

Her lips pressed together, Chloe glanced around the bar. When she was finished, she leaned closer to him. "Is this place clean?"

Ric put a hand on his chest. "Hunt and I scan it regularly. No leaks."

She sighed. "I hate to add fuel to your already diluted theories, but I have heard some of the managers mention something called a Consortium." She sat upright. "But that doesn't mean anything, Ulrich."

He stared at a spot on the bar and waved a hand at her. "Right, right. That's just very interesting."

"I knew I shouldn't have said anything."

"Hey. I get it. It's all hearsay and rumours. Nothing definitive. I just." He scratched his head. "I've been trying to raise my profile, get more legitimate jobs and I like to know as much as I can."

"All done," Hunt said. "You're clean. And might I say, you've got some really neat components—"

"Hunt!" Ric clenched his teeth. "Sorry."

Chloe smiled. "It's okay. I guess he's still a bit of a kid."

"Sometimes." Concentrating on the projection

in his left eye, the rest of the tavern went fuzzy. "Hunt, how about a rundown."

"You got it."

A list of Chloe's components scrolled past with a status next to each one. There was regular wear and minor data corruption standard with any heavy use implants, and the date for the next scheduled reset. Ric squinted at it, scrolling through the data several times. "I don't see any issue with your components." Blinking, he faded out the projection and her face came into focus. "There're traces of corruption, but well within tolerance." He rubbed his shoulder. "A full reboot couldn't hurt, but the tremors aren't from your synthetic parts."

Chloe frowned. "It's not rejection sickness."

He shook his head. "I'm not saying that. But when was the last time you took a break?"

"It's been a while." She crossed her arms.

"Could it be stress? You're unconsciously controlling a lot of synthetics and your nervous system gets a ton of feedback." He half-smiled. "If you're burning the midnight oil, you could just be overwhelmed."

"So, what? I should take a vacation?"

"I'm no doctor and I don't know what your life is like. All I can say for sure is that from this scan, there is nothing wrong with your implants."

Chloe clenched her jaw and her foot bounced

rapidly.

"Can I give you a suggestion?"

"Fine."

"If you can manage it, see a doctor for a real physical." He shrugged.

"It's not that easy." Standing, Chloe headed for the door. She stopped before pushing it open.

Ric counted to five in his head. "I didn't say it was."

She turned back to face him. "If I see a doctor then everyone will know there is something wrong with me and I'll be labeled as defective." Clenching her fists, her irises opened and closed, as if she were struggling to focus on him. "What little clout I've earned will be gone. Even if I get out of it un-scathed, if I take any time off someone else will just take my place." Her bottom lip trembled. "Then what?"

"I don't know." Ric fought the urge to stand and go to her. "But if you don't do anything, you'll get... worse."

She took a step farther into the tavern and one of the people sleeping in the back yawned and rus-tled around. Chloe pulled a credit chip out of her jacket pocket and tossed it in Ric's direction. "Here."

He watched it fall to the floor between them. Sighing, he stood and picked it up. "I don't want—" Straightening to hand it back to her he saw the door swing shut. She hurried past the dirty window as the sun dipped behind one of the mammoth skyscrapers, plunging the bar into a second night.

Sneering, he ran after her, slamming into the door with his shoulder. By the time he was outside, she was lost in the crowd of people. Ric stepped up onto the windowsill to get a higher vantage point, but he couldn't see her head peeking above the throng. He watched vendors sell stale produce from stalls along the street, drunks stumbling in and out of taverns and izakaya, the small, covered Japanese eateries.

Ric dropped back down and stomped into The Fish Market. He slapped the credit voucher on the bar. "Tony. Put this towards my tab."

"You sure?" The bartender had cleared away Chloe's mug and was wiping down the spot where she had been sitting. He scooped up the card with a wipe like a magician.

"I gotta go get ready for this job." Ric scratched the bridge of his nose and went to take a sip of his coffee, but the mug was empty.

"I mean about the money." Tony took the mug and reached behind him to put it down in the dishwasher. When he turned back, he had Ric's puffer vest.

"Why let it go to waste?" Ric accepted the worn red vest and slipped it on. "Hopefully the next time

I see her I'll be able to pay her back."

"Hey." Tony grabbed a glass from under the bar and poured a beer. He slid it to the end of the bar in time for one of the drunks to catch it and drain the glass. "I thought your job wasn't until this evening?"

Ric headed for the door. "I want to make sure I can get into the bathroom and get ready. I don't wear suits very often."

"Wanna look professional, eh? Well, good luck." Tony poured another beer. The man at the end of the bar hiccupped. He had one eye closed and seemed to be making himself sick with his own breath. "Good luck," he managed to echo.

FIVE

Good
Samaritan

Ric stuck close to the Wall. The road wasn't full of people like the adjacent streets. He hated what was on the other side of the boarded-up buildings but so did most people. The few folks using the route wouldn't even look towards the huge barrier. A strip of dirt roughly the width of the tavern separated the Wall from the cracked and pitted street.

Kicking at the weeds growing out of the cracks, Ric kept an eye on the monolith. He enjoyed seeing all the mismatched materials and questionable construction that connected the buildings and extended high above them. Occasionally he would spot sentries on the peaks or faces peering out of cracked and barred windows. His brother had told him they were born in the Wall, but Ric didn't have any concrete memories of his time there and preferred to pretend he'd never stepped foot beyond the barrier.

A small bird landed on the brown grass, taking him out of the tought. It twittered and pecked at the dry Earth, taking flight at the sound of crunching gravel when a passerby stepped in a hole in the road.

The intersection Ric took to head back towards the city was the same one that led into the wall. He saw the entrance ahead with a small gathering of merchants trying to attract the attention of the people walking the quiet road and not the armed guards who stood on either side of the arched opening. A figure in what looked like a real leather jacket caught Ric's attention. The man was tall and he held his head high. He seemed to be scanning the street and not whatever his implant showed him.

Ric thought of his brother who was so against implants. A man who would expound the virtues of living in the real world and knowing what threats lurked around every corner. The lanky stranger appeared more like an animal than a citizen of the Eastern Urban Sprawl, like the bird ready to take flight at the next sound.

"Hey, Ric," Hunt said.

"Yeah?" Ric whispered, moving his lips as little as possible.

"That guy you're looking at. The one that looks like a stranger."

Smiling at the description the AI had used that perfectly encapsulated what he was thinking, Ric brushed his hair back. "What about him?"

"He has cerebral damage from forced implant ejection. He's suffering from leakage."

Ric looked away and crossed the street to be closer to his turn. "How can you tell?"

"I may have been using the local network cameras and checking out people with the different visual modes."

His pace faltering, Ric huffed and pressed on. "That's too bad."

"Well, we have to help him, right?" Hunt said.

As they got closer, Ric switched to typing his side of the conversation on his thigh. *What are we supposed to do? I can't fix brain damage.*

"You taught me to help people." Hunt's voice sounded urgent and it caused a flood of adrenaline in Ric's system. "My programming and the Cardinal Tenets won't let me ignore a person on the verge of dying."

He's not on the verge of anything other than walking into the Wall, which is, I'll grant you, bad.

"But if we don't do anything he will."

Ric clenched his teeth and vigorously scratched his scalp with both hands. *If I go and tell him to avoid the Wall and go to a clinic, will you drop it?*

"Yes."

The memory of his brother smiling after winning an argument made Ric grimace. He changed directions and jogged towards the opening into the Wall. Holding up his hands, he ignored the merchants and caught up to the man. He grabbed the guy's leather jacket and faltered, the feel of it catching him off guard. "Uh."

Up close, the man looked pallid. His waxy complexion made the circles under his eyes stand out.

"Hey, man." Ric let go of the jacket. The stranger's stare made him hesitate. "That's not a great place in there for, uh, people not from... there."

"Great job," Hunt said.

The man blinked slowly and swallowed. Ric noticed a bit of red staining the corner of his mouth.

"Look, the Wall is dangerous and really hard to get through. If you can avoid it, you should." He shrugged and started to turn away.

"The brain damage!" said Hunt.

Ric rubbed the bridge of his nose with the back of his hand. "Right. Also, you have some cerebral damage from implant ejection. There's signs of leakage, too. You should go to a clinic as soon as you can or—yeah."

The man squinted, as if he were staring at the sun. "Where?" His mouth was tight and the words sounded strained.

"There's one just a few blocks from here." Ric pointed down the road, away from the Wall then jerked his thumb to the left.

Hunt hummed.

Ric tried to ignore it. "If you turn at the izakaya selling fried takoyaki, you should find it."

Hunt got louder.

"I don't have money," the man said.

His eye twitching, Ric smiled. He typed to Hunt while answering the man. *Cut it out.* "They sometimes trade for service or you might be able to convince someone to help you out."

Giving up on the humming, Hunt switched to loud sighs.

"Thank you." The man limped away, one foot dragging.

"We should at least show him where the clinic is," said Hunt.

We did enough. I have to get ready for the Mahoney job.

"That's not for hours!"

Ric clenched his teeth. *Fine, but that's it. We show him where it is then we go. Last time we were there, the doctor told me not to come back unless I was bleeding to death.* With the conversation over, the merchants swarmed him again. One of the guards had lifted his visor made from half of an old welding mask and was stiffly walking towards them. Ric pushed through the gathering crowd and hurried to the limping man. Catching up to him for a second time, Ric brushed back his bangs again. "Hey, I was guilted into showing you where the clinic is."

The man nodded.

Ric led the man down the busy sidewalks that overflowed into the equally packed streets where small cars, motorbikes, and delivery vehicles inched forward through the crowd like they were fording a river.

They took another turn through a dirty alley, Ric straining against the slow pace. He clapped his hands together. "So, where're you from?"

"North."

Ric snorted. "I guessed that much since you were about to go in the Wall. But you can't be from around here if you were willing to actually go in there."

"I know. I was in there yesterday."

"Really?" Ric raised an eyebrow. "I don't know if it's brave or stupid. Hey." Sidestepping, he kept pace with the limping man. "You didn't happen to see a ship fly overhead while you were in there, did you?"

The man nodded.

"No way. I heard something about that, but it's not normal. In fact I don't think I've ever seen it happen before—and I've lived around here most of my life." Ric smiled. "So, where north? Like, farther than Chinorth?"

"North of the city."

Ric grimaced. "I guess I'll take your word for it.

So, what's your name anyway?"

They pushed into the next street, Ric doing his best to clear the way for the injured man.

The guy swallowed and leaned closer. "Zed."

Ric stopped, people bumping into him. "Did you say—" Managing to not say the name out loud, he mouthed it.

"Yes." The man looked down at him, breathing hard.

"That's a bad joke." Ric turned away. Instantly turning back, he pointed a finger at the man. "Some people would shoot you just for saying that name, not that I believe in ghosts."

Ignoring the dirty looks from other pedestrians, Ric got moving again. "Is that really your name? Like for real?"

"Yes. It has been a burden."

"I'll bet." Ric frowned. "We're almost there." He nodded to a sign hanging over the sidewalk up ahead. The white cross on the green background identified the place as a clinic.

Several people with various injuries and illnesses clustered around the door. The ones who could walk swarmed them like flies around a dumpster. They pushed each other out of the way to get closer, even more desperate than the merchants near the entrance to the Wall.

Ric held his breath and kept his elbows up, lead-

Break/Interrupt

ing Zed into the tiny storefront.

SIX
Cold Front

The door emitted an electronic chime as it closed behind them. None of the desperate sick followed. There was a counter to the left with a sliding frosted glass window and ahead of them, a door that led farther into the building. A row of filthy, stained chairs along the right side of the room were empty but a woman stood near them with a swollen belly as if she were ready to give birth any moment.

"They should be able to help you here," Ric said. He leaned closer to Zed's ear. "Don't tell them you can't pay. If you do, they won't help you, but once they've treated you, they might be willing to barter."

Zed swallowed hard. "Is there another way?"

The window at reception slid open and a woman was sitting at the desk. She waved at the pregnant woman. "Go on in, sweetie. Room four."

Ric froze with his back to her. "I'd better go.

They're not fond of me here even though I'm paid up," he whispered.

"I can tell that's you Ulrich, and the doctor won't see you without money up front."

Mouthing a curse word, he screwed on his fake smile and spun on his toes. "Nurse Litvin. I'm not the one in need of assistance today, so there is no need to worry." He gestured to Zed like a salesman showing off a new car. "This poor gentleman on the other hand is dying and we wouldn't want that on our hands, would we?"

"What did you do to him?"

"I didn't do anything." His shoulders dropped. "I stopped this guy from going into the Wall and he happens to have a hole in his head. I'm just trying to do something nice."

"Uh huh." Litvin reached through the window and tapped at a scanner built into the wall next to it. "Why don't you come here and let me see what's wrong," she said to Zed.

Zed looked to Ric then limped to the scanner. He flinched when the beam of green light shone on his feet and climbed up to his head. When it reached the top of its path, it dropped back to his face and turned red.

Litvin scrunched her nose. "Yeah. That's pretty bad."

"See." Ric shrugged.

46

"I can fit him in today, but no one is going through that door until the treatment has been paid for."

"If this guy dies, it's on your hands." Ric went for the exit.

Hunt said, "You can't!"

"Not our problem, Hunt," Ric mumbled facing the door and the desperate people pressed against it. "We can't help everyone."

"We can help Zed. He seems nice, and if we leave the clinic to pay for it, they won't have enough money to help someone else who needs it."

Ric slapped his thigh. "Fine." Turning to the counter, he walked stiffly over to nurse Litvin. "Fine! What's the damage?"

"For a procedure like this," she looked up and away, checking something on her personal projection, "two hundred and fifty."

"Great." Ric tensed, fighting frustration. He sent the allotted credits to the chip embedded in his palm and pressed it against the scanner next to the window.

"That was nice," Hunt said.

That was half our rent for the month. He typed to the AI.

The inner door clicked. "You know the way." Litvin smiled. "Room three."

Zed stared at Ric like a lost child.

"Right. Got it. Fantastic." He opened the door and held it for Zed to follow. The hallway on the other side was narrow and they had to sidestep to the third door. It was open, but Ric slid it shut behind them. There was a reclining seat with some last generation medical tech built into it. Arms extended from the back of it and dangled overhead. Ric gestured to it, and Zed sat, crouching under the lowest appendages. There was another chair next to a small counter with a sink, but it was as dirty as the ones in the waiting room, so Ric stood, leaning against the wall.

He brushed back his hair and checked the timer counting down to his job. "Nothing to worry about. Short wait for the doctor, a quick cleaning and patch-up followed by a simple injection of short-term nanites, and we'll be out of here."

Zed furrowed his brow. "I don't know what that means."

Ric sighed. "The doctor will go in the hole behind your ear and clean out the leakage left by the implant. She'll close the hole and inject you with a small number of tiny robots that will help repair any damage."

At the mention of the robots, Zed's eyes went wide and his gaze flicked to the door.

"Don't worry about it." Ric went to his side. "It's really no big deal. The nanites are non-replicating.

They are so small, they float in your blood like your cells, stop at the damaged area, repair it, and head to the bladder to be," he raised an eyebrow, "peed out. If they don't break down first and dissolve." Putting his hand on the stranger's arm, Ric remembered trying to convince his brother that the implants were safe. "I've had nanite injections half-a-dozen times. I do full body scans every month for maintenance," he rolled up his sleeve to show the port and cable retracted into his forearm, "and I'm perfectly okay."

The sound of footsteps passed by in the hallway, and Ric pulled his sleeve down. Zed looked at the spot then up to his eyes.

Ric pressed his shoulder, feeling the compute-unit. "Implants are common, but people like me, with…more are not always treated nicely. I have an AI, an artificial intelligence that I created that lives in a computer in my shoulder. It helps me with my work."

"I suppose I shouldn't make assumptions."

"I think I know what you mean." Ric smiled.

Zed leaned to see past him and furrowed his brow. Ric turned and saw point of light in the wall where he had been standing. It was glaring, bright even in the examination room. It started about half-a-metre above his head, cut through the wall in a straight line, then moved down to the floor. The section of the wall pushed inward and a blast of cold rushed into the tiny room. Flakes of snow rode the wind and fluttered to the floor in a swirl.

"Hunt?" The section of wall swung towards Ric like a door.

"I don't know what's happening."

A hooded figure stood in the impossible doorway. He was slightly shorter than Ric. The space beyond was dark with pale shafts of light streaming through gaps in broken stone walls. There was snow on the ground and piled up in shadowy corners. As his eyes adjusted, Ric noticed more doors, the snow disturbed in front of some of them.

He swallowed and stepped fully in front of the figure as tall as he could. "Who are you?"

"Tom. Who are you?"

"Ulrich."

Tom reached out, making him jump, but the figure grabbed a knob that Ric hadn't noticed.

Ric held the door open. "What do you want?"

"I'm looking for a way home." Tom kept his hand on the knob, but didn't try to force the door closed.

"Where's home?"

"Earth." Tom let go of the knob and backed up a step. He held out a robed hand as if he were aiming a weapon.

Ric held out his own hand like he would to a scared animal. Like he had to Zed. "This is Earth."

Tom shook his head. "It's not the right one. I have to go."

Ric felt the unit in his shoulder whir and pictured his brother's dirty face as he rounded up other kids on the street and brought them in from the cold. "Can I help?"

Tom sniffed. "No." After a moment, he grabbed the doorknob again. "I have to go."

Ric realized he was still holding the door—or section of wall turned into a door—and let go. "Sorry."

Tom inclined his head and his hood slipped back revealing the face of a boy, a teenager at the most.

Before the door closed completely, Ric lunged for the shrinking gap. "Good luck."

With another moving point of light, the door disappeared. Ric felt the wall, picking at it with his fingernails where the seam had been, but there was nothing there.

The door to the hallway slid open and both men screamed.

Break/Interrupt

SEVEN

Ignore The Strange

The doctor jumped. She put one hand to her chest and the other on the doorframe. Ric was standing in a small mound of melting snow.

"Ric?" Straightening her coat, she reached back and pulled her ponytail out of her collar. Her hair was chocolate brown with small streaks of pink and blue running the length of it. "What the hell is going on here?"

"Doctor Lopez." Ric kicked a clump of snow off of his canvas sneakers. "That's a great question." He scooped up handfuls of the stuff and dropped it into the sink. Pulling free a wad of paper towels, he wiped the wet floor. "I don't have an answer, but I'm here with this gentleman who is in need of some serious help."

"Where did the snow come from?" Lopez watched a few remaining flakes float to the floor.

"Uh." Ric stopped, towels dripping in his hands. "The wall opened up and there was a guy—a kid really. He was in another dimension and it was night and snowing."

Lopez rubbed the bridge of her nose. "I would give you a brain scan, but I don't have the time and you don't have the money. Also, I wouldn't care except for the fact that you brought snow in my exam room for some reason."

Ric stood, dropping the wet mess in the trash, and wiped his hands on his pants. "I did clean it, so."

With a sigh, the doctor went to the exam chair. "Let's see what we have here." She quickly turned to stare at Ric, her ponytail swinging. "You did pay up front?"

He leaned against the counter. "Ask Litvin."

"Well." She pressed her lips together and went back to Zed. "There is some cleanup to do."

"How long do you think it'll take?" Ric asked.

"Not long. Twenty minutes—half-hour at the most." She left the chair and went to the sink.

Ric moved out of her way and stood in the still open doorway. "Right. And how long until he'll be good to go?"

With her hands washed, she returned to the chair. "There's a sprain in the ankle and some bruises and abrasions. Plus you managed to bite a hole nearly through your tongue. Nothing worth surgery." She patted Zed's shoulder. "Rest is the cheapest and still one of the best remedies. Unless one of you wants to pay the fee for direct injected nanites."

Ric guffawed. "I'm tapped."

Lopez directed Zed to roll onto his side so she had access to the hole in his head. She grabbed one of the instruments dangling from the arms over the chair. "You can stay if you want, but don't bother me while I'm poking around inside someone's brain."

"Got it." Ric checked the time and the countdown on his projection.

Doctor Lopez hunched over Zed and turned on the instrument she was holding. There was a faint whistling sound that pitched up and down as she manipulated the arm.

Ric closed his eyes and brought up a simple version of the VR Enclave Maze. *Wanna play a game?*

"Sure, but can we start with the handicap this time?" Hunt asked. "We're going to use it eventually and the games are too easy without it."

Easy for you. Ric rocked his head side to side. *Fine, but we're starting with a low one. I need to keep sharp.*

They played a dozen games, each one with an increased difficulty for Hunt. Ric made their final match last almost ten minutes before being beaten by the AI. When Hunt claimed the last tunnel to make winning mathematically impossible, Ric scrunched up his face.

Shit. I thought I had you.

"You almost did, but I noticed you had been rushing in the previous games, so I guessed correctly that you were setting me up for a trap. Still, that was a good challenge."

Right. Huffing, Ric brushed back his hair. *At a ten-point handicap.*

"That's really good for a non-AI. Also, I think the doctor is finished. The sound of that device stopped."

Ric opened his eyes and recoiled at the glare in the exam room. Lopez was leaning backwards, her hands on her lower back.

"All done?" He took her cue and stretched his arms.

"Just about." She went to the sink and washed her hands again. "I think I got all the leakage and I closed the hole. The nanites will get anything I may have missed as they repair the actual damage." She walked up to him at the doorway. "Excuse me."

He backed into the hall and she headed farther into the clinic.

"Just need to get a syringe of nanites and code their instructions."

Going back into the room, he went to the chair. "Hey. How ya doing?"

Zed was sitting upright. He put his fingers to the spot behind his ear. "A little groggy, but much better."

"Well, after you get those nanites and some pain meds, you'll be laughing." He leaned on the armrest. "I've been thinking. You have a long trip ahead of you and if you don't cross the Wall, it's going to take a long time. I'm going to be making a bunch of credits tonight." He rubbed his nose. "I want to pay for a transport to take you directly to the north end of the city. They can fly you around the wall and get you there in a matter of days instead of weeks, or—hell, I'm not even sure how far north the city goes."

Zed shook his head once and stopped, grimacing. "I couldn't accept. You have already been too generous."

Ric brushed his hair back. "Look, just let me help you. I won't be able to concentrate on my job tonight if I'm worried about you in the damn Wall or walking around it on your way home. It's not that much money and like I said, I'm coming into a fair bit tonight."

"I can't." Zed looked away.

"I understand. I really do. We loners have stupid pride getting in our way and to be honest, I probably wouldn't have helped you in the first place if it wasn't for the AI in my shoulder bugging me about it. If I don't help you get home, he'll never let me hear the end of it. Please."

"I have no way to repay you."

"Seriously, don't worry about it. This is my good deed for the decade. And if it bothers you that much, you can pay back some other person in need. My brother used to say it all comes around."

Lopez came back into the room and Ric moved out of her way. She carried a white plastic case and he could see the outline of a syringe behind the opaque material.

The doctor pulled a cable from the chair and plugged it into the case. A faint glowing light changed from white to red. She dragged and pointed in the air, interacting with her implant and when she finished, the light at the bottom of the case changed to green and slowly took over the red.

Ric knew from his own experience with injections that the changing colour illustrated the progress of the coded instructions of the microscopic robots in the syringe.

When the entire case was green, Lopez cracked a seal on the side and it split open. She dropped the remnants into a chute in the wall to be wiped and recycled. "Back on your side," she said to Zed. "I have to inject this close to the site if you want it to be effective."

Pulling back his collar, she stuck the needle into his neck and slowly depressed the plunger.

Ric looked away.

"All done." Lopez tossed the syringe in the same chute and stuck a little round bandage on the tiny puncture. Pushing on Zed's arm, she prompted him to roll back over then helped him get out of the chair. "You shouldn't feel any side effects, but you're pretty beat up and even with the help, that hole in your head will take a lot of healing. You should rest for at least a week. That means no lifting, no running, no working, and stay in bed as much as you can." She nodded curtly and went to wash her hands. "I wish I could let you stay here for a while, but space is at a premium."

"Thanks, Doc," Ric said.

Lopez went into the hallway. "I should be thanking you. Helping a stranger and paying for it." She grinned. "Maybe you do need a brain scan." Leaving the door open, she headed off to another room and another patient.

Zed stood by the chair slowly rocking back and forth.

"You'll be fine. We should go." Ric put a hand on his back and guided him out of the exam room. "Though I bet you aren't going to forget your first time in a clinic. It was a new one for me with that supernatural door."

Zed stopped. "It was the giants."

Ric furrowed his brow. "Giants?"

"You can't see them in the city. It's too loud, too busy." He squinted at Ric, his hand on the wall. "Much easier in the forest, but they are here. They guide us. Talk to us. Them and the ghosts, but don't trust the ghosts."

"You know, yesterday I would have called you nuts, but after that." Ric gestured behind him. "What the hell do I know?" He nodded towards the exit. "Come on, I have to get you to a transport and go get ready for my appointment. And no arguing. You heard the doctor, you need the rest."

EIGHT
Diverging Paths

Ric led Zed back to the busy street. They stayed on the south side and continued past storefronts and stalls, pushing through the ever-present crowds. They stopped at an izakaya serving yakitori, skewers of chicken and vegetables, to grab a bite and let Zed rest a bit.

Several more blocks south and east, they reached a building that would have been called a skyscraper before the gigantic street straddling behemoths were built. It was a concrete structure with large windowsills and ornate filigree, including a surviving gargoyle with a long eroded expression.

Together, Ric and Zed shouldered their way through a revolving door, timing their impacts to get it to rotate, and traversed the lobby—empty except for debris and trash.

Riding the elevator to the top floor, they wandered down twisting hallways following arrows printed on computer paper and stuck to the walls with tape. Some of them had fallen off, but Ric mostly remembered the route and they got to the metal staircase to the roof without having to back-track.

The wind lashed out at them as soon as the door was open. There was a waist-high wrought-iron fence with bent and missing bars around the perimeter of the roof and a chain-link fence beyond it, sticking out of the sides of the building at an angle. In the middle of the otherwise open space was a raised platform with another short metal staircase. On top, Ric could see the small craft and behind it a tiny cinderblock building.

There was a short antenna jutting out of the small structure with a light that alternated blinking red and green slowly enough for Ric to keep misjudging the timing. The wind blew his shaggy hair into his face and after several failed attempts to fix it, he held it in place with a hand.

They walked up to the platform and around the ship. The vehicle was not much larger than the vans that travelled along the roads, but it had stubby wings running the length of it with engine ports arching from the them in a single piece. Burn marks around welded spots, streaks of filth from flying through polluted clouds, and several dings adorned the two-tone exterior—baby blue on the top half and silver on the bottom separated by a navy pinstripe.

A man came out of the door-less opening in the side of the shack, holding down his captain's hat.

He was taller than either of them with broad shoulders under a leather jacket as worn as Zed's, but being synthetic it was more tattered with spots where the fake leather had flaked off. Wisps of hair sticking out of his hat, salt and pepper like his beard, danced in the churning air currents.

Hiking up his pants as he approached, he yelled over the wind. "What brings you here, kid?"

"Got a passenger for you, Paulie. Long trip around the wall and as north as you go." Ric walked past the man and into the cinderblock hut. He forcefully ran his hands through his hair one after the other, desperate to get it out of his face.

Ducking under the doorway, Paulie took two long steps to a wheeled office chair and dropped into it. The chair creaked as he leaned back and scooted away from the control board set up on a desk made from scrap wood across stacked cinderblocks.

Zed stopped just inside and leaned against the wall.

"Not too much weight there." Paulie pointed at the wall. "The concrete holding this place together isn't doing its job so well anymore."

Ric stepped over a low table made the same way

as the desk and sat on a couch that looked as if it were once part of an older ship, complete with seat-belts. He gestured for Zed to join him. "Hey, Paulie, you lost weight?"

The man grinned broadly. "Ah, you trying to butter me up for something, kid?"

"No, I mean it."

Paulie stuck out his chin. "As a matter of fact, I've been on a new diet. Lost fifteen pounds."

"Good for you." Ric checked the time. It was afternoon, but he didn't need to rush. "So, Paulie. About that trip."

The pilot pulled at the waist of his pants. "Yeah, around the Wall and north, right? I'm willing to go all the way to the outskirts of the city, but it's still growing, ya see." He held his hands out as far apart as he could. "North and south. I haven't been to the edge in a while, so I can't say for sure how far that's going to be."

Ric raised an eyebrow. "Give me an estimate and I'll add a little bonus in case it's farther than you guess."

Bringing the side of his fist to his mouth, Paulie burped into it. "Well, let me see." He spun in the chair, grabbed a tattered notebook from the desk, and scooted back around to face them scanning the pages. "Trip to the northern edge of the city. Single passenger, that's an extra fee at the tolls, plus new pollution surcharges. Danger pay for going around the Wall, payoff to the northern gangs for crossing their territories." He clicked his tongue. "It's not going to be cheap, kid."

"How am I not surprised?" Ric stood. "Look. This guy's already guilty enough that I paid his fee at the clinic, could you tone down the price gouging and get to it?"

Putting the notebook down, Paulie grabbed a handful of nuts from a bin on the floor next to him. He shuffled them around in his hand and tossed one into his mouth. "What're you doing going around playing hero? That thing in your head making you go squirrely or did your brother come back and scold you for being a sensible person?"

"It doesn't matter." Ric crossed his arms. "Can we get to the point, because I have a gig to get to tonight and I'm going to need to make it on time if I'm going to be able to pay you for this."

"Alright, kid." Paulie dropped the nuts into the bin and rubbed his hands together. "No need to get your undies in a bunch. When do you want to do this?"

"Now, right?" Ric glanced at Zed who nodded.

Paulie grunted, rocking forward and pushing on the armrests to stand. The chair slid into the makeshift desk and the man kept grumbling as he straightened. He looked over to Zed. "In that case.

If you don't mind making a few stops for cheap fuel and some personal reasons of my own that I will not divulge. Do not ask." He squinted and held his hands up as if ready to physically deflect a question. "I can leave now and I'll even cut you a deal. Say, three hundred credits?"

"You're a dirty cheat!" Ric pointed at the older man.

"Hey." Paulie puffed out his chest. "I have a business to run."

"You have people to steal from, you mean." Walking right up to him, Ric clenched his jaw and met his gaze.

"You have no idea how far it is to the edge of the city, kid!" Paulie spread out his arms and looked from side to side. "We're just about as smack dab in the middle as you can be. It'll take two—three days, easy."

"You mean with those personal stops you intend to make along the way."

"Maybe, but between fuel and paying off gangs to fly over their territories, wear on my ship, Corporate tolls, and my license," the pilot ticked off the points on his fingers, "three hundred will barely cover it."

Ric walked away, shaking his head. "You used to be cool, Paulie."

"That's a low blow, kid!" Paulie sneered. "You

have no idea what it's like to be the cock-of-the-walk one day and over-the-hill the next."

"Fine!" Ric waved his hands like a person desperately trying to flag a taxi in the rain. When Paulie didn't rebut, he fixed his hair. "How about Hunt and I do a full system scan and I help you make some upgrades to your ship's code when you get back?"

"And the three hundred credits?"

"One-fifty."

"Okay, but you do the work now, before we go."

"I have a job to get to."

Paulie sighed. "Fine. It's a deal, kid. But you better not make me have to track you down when I get back." He clapped his hands together and smiled. "Alright, guy I've never met before. Let's get in the air."

Zed got to his feet gingerly. "I'm Zed."

Ric dashed to Paulie and put his hands against the man's chest. "Paulie. Wait! Don't!"

"Zed?" The man took a step, easily pushing Ric with him.

"It's an unfortunate coincidence." Ric grunted as he gave up on pushing and stood in-between them. "He's not even from the city."

The pilot snorted. "A hundred and seventy-five."

Ric stopped pushing. "Okay, but on one condition."

"What?"

"If, when you come back, you're still mad at this guy for, let's be real, an unlucky name, then I'll pay you the extra twenty-five."

Paulie glowered at the lanky outsider standing between the couch and the coffee table then looked down at Ric. "You're sure about this?"

Ric shrugged. "It's not his fault."

Without a word, Paulie turned and headed outside. Before following, Ric stopped Zed. "Nothing about ghosts or giants, okay?"

Zed nodded and they left the little building.

There was a rumble over the howl of the wind as the ship started. Black clouds of smoke blasted out of the exhaust ports and were whipped away, replaced by clear gas that made heat-lines in the air. The door on the side of the ship was open.

Coming from the cockpit, Paulie crouched just inside and pointed to a pile of boxes and bags stacked against the cinderblock wall. "Little help?"

Ric and Zed relayed the cargo to the pilot. When they were done, Paulie helped Zed climb onto the wing and inside the ship.

"You'd better get off the platform, kid," he yelled.

Ric waved. "Thanks again, Paulie. I'll transfer the money on the way to the street."

The pilot nodded and moved out of view. The door started to slide closed. Zed was strapped into a seat, surrounded by the bags and boxes. He looked pale, but when he saw Ric, he inclined his head. "Thank you!"

As soon as the stranger was blocked from view, Ric hurried around the ship, down the steps, and across the roof. He went to the enclosure at the corner of the building and stood by the door, watching the ship lift off.

It moved slowly at first, rocking slightly in the high winds, then it shot forward towards the nearest stream of flying vehicles heading west towards the harbor.

Break/Interrupt

NINE
What Makes A Man

Squinting at the bright sunshine sliding from behind a skyscraper, Ric backed through the doorway. While riding down the elevator, he transferred the credits to Paulie's account. He shoved his way out of the building, eventually squeezing through the tight gap in the revolving door. Once outside, he joined the flow of people that was going in the same direction as his apartment.

"That was an interesting side-quest," Hunt said.

Ric glanced up and to the left, as if he were on a call through his implant. "That wasn't a side-quest, it was a detour. A waste of time."

"But we helped someone. Zed would have died."

Grimacing, Ric brushed back his hair. "Let's not use his name so openly."

"Why not? No one can hear us. Well, no one can hear me."

"Don't make it a habit of saying that name. You've seen how people react to it."

"I don't have habits. I have code," Hunt said with a giggle. "I can't slip up. If I'm ordered to not say that name, I just don't. Unless there is an error in my code and at the risk of being immodest, my code is the best."

"I'll take that as a compliment." Breaking free from the crowd, Ric pushed his way to an alley. "Though, by now, the code I wrote is a minor part of your personality."

"That's not true. It's at my core. That's like a human's genetic traits or automatic brain functions. I don't think about them, but they happen and are a key component of how I've developed."

"Well, here's to that." Ric crossed the next street, narrowly avoiding being hit by a motorcycle that was weaving between pedestrians. He cut down another alley and reached the back of his building. Taking the fire escape, he climbed up to the eighth floor and in through the propped-open fire exit. He'd given up worrying about building security after his first week and focused on keeping his tiny apartment safe.

The wood floor creaked under his footfalls, the sound mixing with the various noises leaking out of the doors he passed and the ever-present clamor of the city. He wrinkled his nose at the sour smell that, while worse on damp days, was as relentless as the din. Most of the compact and crammed together apartments had cameras hanging over their doors, but Ric had written an algorithm to blur his face on their recordings and Hunt had dropped the code into everyone's networks.

The AI jumped into the apartment's system and started the process of unlocking the door.

The lock clicked open and Ric stepped over the threshold, closing the door behind him. He sighed and took off his vest, hanging it in the open space that was as close as he had to a closet. Made out of sections of the neighbouring apartment, the room was slightly deeper than it was wide, with a single window at the back that Ric had covered with tinfoil. While the free floor space was almost big enough for him to lie down comfortably, it was just tall enough for him to have added a second level—at a sacrifice to headroom. A ladder attached to the wall led up to a loft with enough height for him to sit.

There was a counter with a sink and tiny fridge on the first floor, though his server and storage unit took up a quarter of the space. Fans in the setup spun, pumping out heat. Status lights blinked in complex patterns.

"Hunt, can you please see if there is a free timeslot for the bathroom?"

"It's free right now. I can book it."

"Thanks." Ric nodded. The bathroom was

shared with the apartment to the left. He and his neighbour had worked out a system for booking time that, for the most part, worked. Ric had considered adding a toilet to his apartment but he didn't like the proximity to his food. He yawned as he went to the closet and dug out the garment bag containing his one suit, two dress shirts, and three ties. "Any activity in the storage tower?"

"Nope. It's pretty quiet in there. Our current tenants aren't too active by nature."

Still holding the hanger, Ric went to the readout on his network hub and checked the activity list. "I guess we'd better pass them along to one of the rehab places."

"Do you think it's worth it for such simple AI?"

Ric furrowed his brow. "What should I do, just delete them?"

"They aren't very sophisticated." Hunt sighed. "At most, they could be put to use combing data, but they'll never be as fast as a dedicated algorithm."

Shrugging, Ric blanked the screen. "But algorithms are so biased. That's how the first blackout happened. Algorithms in charge of too much with inherently flawed architecture." He scooped up his toiletry bag from a shelf by the door and a towel hanging underneath. "At least AI can learn and make up for flawed premises in their base code." Closing his left eye, he logged into the camera over his doorway and scanned the hallway. The coast was clear, so he left his apartment and walked the few steps to the bathroom.

The room was made of a single piece of beige molded plastic except for the two doors, which had covers that slid over them and sealed watertight for the less than stellar automated cleaning cycle.

There was a sink that jutted out of the wall in-between the two doors and a mirror above it—the only permanent fixture not made of the same plastic. On the back wall were the toilet and a built-in cabinet for dry goods. The remaining wall was completely taken up by the shower stall. The space under the sink had two locked compartments, one for each of the users, but Ric tended to take his things with him. The room had no sharp angles or corners and he always thought it looked kind of organic, like the inside of a boring alien.

He hung the garment bag and towel on hooks molded into the wall and dropped his canvas bag on the counter.

"What's my time, Hunt?" Ric stripped and got into the shower stall. He turned on the water with a command over his implant and it sprayed out at his preset temperature.

"You have thirty minutes scheduled in the bathroom and two hours until your meeting." The AI cleared a throat he didn't have. "Can we continue our discussion about the rogue AI in the storage tower?"

Ric scrubbed his hair and thought about booking a haircut. "I just don't feel comfortable deleting AI no matter how basic they are."

"Even the bad ones?"

"That's a whole philosophical argument that I'm not sure I am capable of getting into." Sucking in a mouthful of water, he spat it out like a fountain. "I don't believe there are bad AI. Someone had to program them that way."

"But you always say that my personal growth is more responsible than the core programing you wrote for me."

"Sure, but you also have the Cardinal Tenets playing a role. Most of the rogue AI we've caught don't."

"Most of the rogue AI haven't been raised either."

Ric finished rinsing off his body and stepped out of the shower. The water turned off automatically. "What do you mean?"

"You postulate that I am in control of my development, but you are here to guide me. You tell me right from wrong, suggest paths for study and create challenges that promote growth. You're like a parent. You give me certain freedoms and limitations creating an environment for me to flourish. Most rogue AI are coded and set loose to accomplish the single task they have been given."

Having toweled off, Ric wrapped it around his waist and went to the sink. He took an electric razor from his bag and shaved off his stubble. "I guess I haven't thought about it that way." He paused, pulling his cheek taut. "But if that's the case, wouldn't the AI we captured be in need of a chance to grow? You could almost say they are deserving of it."

"You see them from the perspective of a human with inherent fallacies and tendencies. Like seeing patterns or confirmation bias. You personify them."

"You're probably right, but even if they are simple or don't have human level intelligence, I believe they are sentient. Or sentient enough to deserve a chance."

"That thinking isn't very logical. It costs you money to have a rehab or long-term storage place take them."

"I'd rather be able to sleep at night, even if I can't convince you why it matters to me." Ric went back to shaving.

"You're the boss. I just voiced my opinion."

"Sure. And I'm glad you did, but I'm still going to transfer them to a rehab place. Could you see if anyone has an opening?" Turning off the razor, Ric noticed two gouges in the wall under the mirror. He leaned in closer to take a look and rubbed one of them with a finger. "I wonder where these came from."

"Oh. The other user did that. She hangs a mirror from there because the built in one is too high."

Ric shoved his electric razor in his bag. "Hunt! Don't tell me you've been spying on her!"

"I'm not spying. I'm securing the perimeter around the apartment. You told me to keep an eye out for things."

"I didn't mean watching a woman in a bathroom. That's perverted."

"But I have no physical desires."

"That doesn't matter, Hunt!" Ric ran his fingers through his bangs and grabbed a fistful of hair. "We just talked about this at the bar this morning. You got to stop snooping around so much." Letting go, he scratched his head then took out a toothbrush and paste. "I know I ask you to snoop sometimes, but that's only when we need to, for security."

"It was for security."

"Well, no more spying on the neighbour." He shuddered. "It's gross. If she tries to hack us, we can stop it."

"Okay. I'll stop, but you're going to have to explain to me why it's right sometimes and not others." Hunt sighed.

"Fine, but not today. We have to keep our minds on the job. I spent most of what we're going to earn already."

"Yeah, you told me not to let you do that again." Ric squeezed toothpaste onto the brush. "Remind me again next time."

Break/Interrupt

TEN
Hand-Me-Down

When he was finished primping, Ric zipped open the garment bag. The suit inside was a simple two-piece in dark grey. He chose the brown shirt and green tie to go with it and dressed. The suit had been his brother's and while it was almost the right length in the sleeves, it was too broad in the shoulders. Futzing with the collar, he scooped up his belongings and went back to his apartment, initializing a cleaning cycle behind him.

Dumping his stuff by the door, Ric dug out his boxed dress shoes tucked into the rafters with other odds and ends like pots and boxes from his electronics.

The shoes were brown and fit because he'd purchased them for himself. They were the first thing he bought with the money from his first cleaner job. Before putting them on, he rubbed them down with the included cloth, using his breath to add moisture.

Once fully dressed, he did a spin. "What do you think, Hunt?"

"Objectively?"

"Emotionally." Ric's smile wavered.

"In that case, you look great!"

His credentials were baked into the chip in his hand and available to his clients via a registry, but Ric tucked his access ID into the breast pocket of his suit anyway. He grinned, patting the thick card through the fabric.

"I think that's everything." Ric glanced around the tiny room. "How's the segregated storage in your compute-unit?"

"Wide open. I've been working on my compression techniques, so I haven't added anything to it since the last time you dumped the contents."

"Great." Ric raised an eyebrow. "Why haven't you mentioned these compression techniques?"

"They're a work in progress. Just something for me to do on my downtime." Hunt pretended to sniff. "Do you have any idea how boring it is when you sleep?"

"I can imagine." Ric opened the door and went into the hallway. "I'd like to look them over when we get some time, if you don't mind."

"Of course not. But let me clean up the code first. You get so mad when I don't follow every little rule."

"It's good practice to follow proper guidelines." Ric waited for the door to cycle through the locking procedure before heading to the elevator. "You have to remember that other people may be using your programs and they're going to have to be able to decipher the code to understand how to integrate it or iterate on it."

"I know."

Sticking out his elbow to hit the button to call the elevator, Ric thought better and pressed it with his pinky. The doors opened and he rode it down to the lobby. "Well, don't rush. You can let me know when you feel comfortable sharing them."

The main floor of the building had also been converted to fit in as many apartments as possible, leaving a hallway from the elevator to the front doors lined floor to ceiling in mailboxes. Ric did a quick check as he passed his, using his implant to connect to the alert software in his designated box. He didn't have any pending deliveries but his brother had sent him a letter when he'd first joined Telbac, and Ric was in the habit of checking every time he went in or out the front door.

A bright wedge of sunlight illuminated the street for three blocks. The light, which sneaked through two nearby towering skyscrapers, showed up around noon and crept down the street until early evening where it was finally choked out.

Pausing on the stoop, Ric let the warmth wash over him before bounding down the steps to the ever-busy street. There were usually fewer people in the bright sun, which he found strange at first, but with the general anxiety over solar radiation and the type of people who lived so close to the Wall, Ric came to think of it as normal. He joined the bustle, his head high in the professional armor of his suit.

Mahoney Semiconductor, his current client, was situated in an industrial park on the east end, near the ocean. Ric headed for the nearest Magtram station to board one of the hanging trains that criss-crossed the city.

A feed appeared in the lower left corner of Ric's projection as Hunt accessed nearby cameras. He saw himself from overhead and behind. The feed rapidly cycled through several more angles and he had to close the window to keep from getting dizzy. "Too much input, Hunt."

"Sorry. I keep forgetting your limitations."

Ric cut through a café and into a plaza next to the stairs for the Magtram station. There was a line down the steps and through the open space, winding around circular concrete basins with fountains or plants inside of them. He joined the line behind a tall woman wearing a long cloak and shoes that gave her an extra boost. A group of teens in clothes far too light for the weather got behind him. They jostled each other and one of them kept running to the nearby fountain to jump off it.

Ric clenched his teeth and closed his left eye, opening access to the camera feeds again. "Slow it down for me, Hunt."

"Sure. I'll split the signal so we can set our own speed."

Taking control of what he was seeing, he took the time to study each feed to get an idea where the cameras were without outright looking for them. When he had their rough position, he set a routine to cycle between them in a pattern that gave him a near constant view of the teens while being able to scan the rest of the plaza for other threats.

"What are you doing?" Hunt asked.

Ric typed out his reply. *Just keeping an eye on things.*

"Okay, but I can do that without limiting the time spent on any one camera feed."

Sometimes it makes more sense to gauge your situation and potential threats, splitting your focus accordingly. You have the benefit of being able to brute force this limited amount of information, but if you find yourself in a situation where there is too much to take in at once, you need to learn to prioritize without forgetting to watch for unknowns. A train arrived in the station carrying a gust of wind with it.

The line shuffled forward as exiting passengers descended the stairs on the opposite side of the street. They got to the sidewalk before the line stopped again. An old man carrying several bags and dragging a cart with a squeaky wheel approached the waiting riders. He was hunched and there were scabs on the top of his bald head.

Overhearing him trying to sell bottled water, respirators, battery packs, and other miscellaneous items to the people ahead of him in line, Ric turned him down with a headshake.

One of the kids behind Ric grabbed the man's cart and dragged it to the fountain. Ric hunched his shoulders and looked away.

"Aren't you going to help him?" Hunt asked.

"What am I supposed to do? I'm not much bigger than they are and they have numbers on their side."

"You have to do something."

"Shit." Ric stepped out of the line and faced the kid with the cart. "Hey. Bring that back!"

The teen, jacket hanging half-off, ripped jeans, and a cap that looked like a simplified version of what Paulie wore, had the cart on the precipice. "What did you say?"

Another one of the kids wearing a similar hat in a different colour and a torn sweatshirt shoved the old man.

Ric darted forward to catch him, but the man was able to stumble into one of the basins and hold on to the rim.

"I said bring that cart back." Ric turned on the kid who shoved the old man. "And you should apologize."

"You should apologize for your face!" The teen in the ripped sweatshirt spat at Ric's feet.

"Yeah!" Another one of them said. "Guy looks like he's wearing daddy's suit, tryin'a be a big man."

Ric grimaced and tried to hide his shaking. "At least I'm not a grubby little kid picking on people in front of my friends because I'm too scared to do it on my own." He took another step towards the teen with the cart. "Now, get off of the fountain and bring that cart back."

The teen who had insulted Ric pulled out a knife. It was short with a serrated edge and a plastic handle like he'd stolen it from his parent's kitchen, but it made Ric flinch.

"That's what I thought," the kid said.

There was a loud bang and everyone ducked. A plume of smoke was dissipating above the old man who held a sawed-off shotgun with the stubby barrel pointing in the air. The gun shook along with his hands.

The teens fled and a few bystanders followed but most of the waiting commuters turned back to stare at the station or whatever their implants were projecting.

Ric stood in place until he saw the old man fall. The gun clattered to the ground and the man landed on his hands and knees. Scooping up the shotgun on his way, Ric stuffed it into one of the man's bags and helped him stand. As the man brushed off his pants, Ric went to get the cart. It had tipped over when the teen dropped it to run and while the contents had spilled out, none of it landed in the fountain.

Dragging the cart with him, Ric gathered up the battery packs and bottles of water, working his way to the old man who was sitting on the edge of the basin where he had fallen.

"I'm sorry about that." Ric rolled the cart next to the man.

"You should be!" The man sneered, showing cracked yellow and black teeth. "Because of you my merchandise is damaged."

"Because of me?" Ric took a step back.

The man pointed a crooked finger at the cart. "I can't sell broken battery packs and none of you stuck-up snobs will buy scuffed up water bottles. Who's going to pay me for this?"

"I was just trying to save you from those punks."

"I'm the one who saved you. If it weren't for me, you'd be a stain on the ground." The man snorted a derisive laugh.

"What?" Ric clenched his teeth.

"Pay me! You disrespectful little shit. You destroyed my stuff, you pay for it."

"You're crazy." Heading back to the line, Ric waved off the man.

"Thief! Wuss!"

The line had resettled, the spot behind the tall woman taken up by whoever was next. The people who bothered to look at Ric as he approached either grimaced, sneered, or shook their heads.

"Right." Ric went to the sidewalk and around the stairs leading to the platform.

"Where are we going?" Hunt asked.

"I'm walking to the next station."

"Really?"

His brow furrowed, Ric joined the pedestrian flow following the elevated track east, towards his destination. "Do me a favour, Hunt? Could you blur me out in any camera feeds that recorded that interaction? You know what? Better make it the whole trip here."

"Sure thing." Hunt sighed. "That was disappointing."

"That's what you get for trying to help someone."

"But what about Zed? That worked out okay, didn't it?"

Ric blew out a puff of air. "Other than costing us a few hundred credits and who knows how much labour working on Paulie's ship."

Break/Interrupt

"I guess."

"Hunt."

"Yes?"

"The cameras, please." Ric scratched his nose and sidestepped something squishy on the sidewalk.

ELEVEN
Mahoney Semiconductor

The imposing glass and steel headquarters for Mahoney Semiconductor looked so similar to all the other walled-off office buildings in the area that the only distinction Ric could find was the gate blocking off the entrance had the Mahoney 'M' logo suspended between every other bar and the full name of the company was adorned on top in curving gold letters.

An automated message told him to swipe his badge or implanted chip and a smaller pedestrian gate opened for him. He walked across the mostly empty parking lot and down the long driveway to the building.

A few rays of the waning sun reflected off the mirrored surface and bathed Ric's path in orange. Raising a hand to shade his face, he made it through the front doors.

Across the expansive lobby there was a waterfall splashing into a pool lined with what looked like a section of stream cut straight out of nature and dropped into the building. The rocks at the bottom caused the water to spray onto the muddy banks, which gave way to grass. There was a tree on the right side and birds tweeting, barely audible over the roar of the water, which churned and flowed to where the banks ended and—

Ric stood in the doorway and squinted at the spot where the stream just ended and the water vanished. He looked up. The lobby was open to the higher floors for as far as he could see and the source of the waterfall was similarly out of sight.

A woman in a dark blue blazer and matching skirt stopped beside him. "Rather remarkable, no?"

"Amazing." Ric tore his gaze away from the quandary and found it hard to look away from her. He brushed back his hair. "I'm, uh. I have an appointment."

"Yes. I know who you are." She smiled, but the gesture didn't reach her eyes. "I have to say I'm disappointed." Frowning, she stuck out her bottom lip like a child.

Ric hesitated. "Why's that?"

"All those implants and so few Mahoney parts." The pout transformed into a tight smile. "I'm sorry. We do like our fun here. You were scanned when you came through the front door." She winked and gestured to the waterfall. "Do you care to guess how it's achieved?"

"Sure." He furrowed his brow. "I thought it might have been grating, or some kind of drain, but the air's dry. And the birds never leave the, uh, illusion." He pointed to them swooping down from the tree and fluttering back. "It's a hologram. The largest scale I've ever heard of."

"Correct, though that information is easy enough to look up for a person of your background. We are proud of our little light show." The woman pursed her lips. "You would have signed a waiver and the confidentiality agreement at the time of hiring, so we may as well get down to business."

Ric nodded. "I'm ready when you are."

She led him around the fake waterfall to the elevators and down to sub-basement three, riding in silence.

When the doors opened, Ric stepped out but the woman stayed in the car.

"Just down that hallway." She pointed past him.

"Uh, thanks." Ric nodded. "I'm sorry, I don't think I got your name?"

"That's right. You didn't."

The doors closed, leaving him alone.

Break/Interrupt

TWELVE
Infiltration

Dazed by the strange woman, Ric shook his head and walked down the long hallway to a set of double doors. When he pushed them open, he was assailed by the sound of shouts, warning alarms, and tramping feet.

He winced as he went farther into the room. There was a central console the size of several dining room tables taking up most of the sunken center of the octagonal space. The walls were lined with standing servers, metal cabinets holding the innards of the vast supercomputer. Across the room was another hallway with glass walls. Ric could see the flashing lights on over a hundred more cabinets.

One of the half-dozen technicians noticed him, climbed the three steps from the middle of the room, and pushed up his glasses. "Who are you?"

"I'm the cleaner." Ric looked past the man to a

large display hanging from the ceiling over the central console. It had four main screens, each facing a cardinal direction, and smaller screens in the corners, mirroring the shape of the room. The screens showed a huge infiltration, lists of infected sectors scrolled by, a diagram of the super computer and the entire Mahoney network had sections bathed in red with flashing points of light illustrating the sites of attack. "I guess that's why I was called."

"Lien told them we don't need any help. We can handle this." The technician fixed his Mahoney branded tie.

"That looks like the start of a cascade failure across your network." Ric pointed to the spreading infection. "Multiple points of entry, as if a few groups got together to organize this. Release a new processor that ruffled the feathers of some hardcore fans?"

"It's under control!" The tech turned and stumbled down the stairs, flopping onto the console.

A woman popped her head out of the hallway at the back of the room. "Is that the guy?"

Ric casually crossed to her and, when he got to the stairs on the opposite side, he leaned against the railing. "Hi. I'm Ric. He said you don't need me." He pointed a thumb over his shoulder toward the tech by the console.

The woman stepped into the lights of the octagonal room and Ric saw she was a few years younger than he was. He guessed maybe nineteen or twenty. Her dark hair was up in a ponytail that arced off the back of her head before gravity could pull the lower strands down into a sharp drop. She had spots of grease on her face and goggles resting on the top of her head. The sleeves of her long blue lab coat were rolled up to her elbow, exposing an interface jack in her forearm and she held a huge red wrench with spots where the colour had been worn off from use.

"Since you're here, I may as well get our money out of you. I'm Lien, head technician." Lowering the wrench, she wiped sweat off her brow, smearing the grease.

"This isn't what I expected, but I'm game." Ric took off his jacket and draped it over the railing. Unbuttoning his sleeves, he rolled them up, exposing his own interface. "Is there a console I can use?"

Lien point with the wrench to the behemoth behind him, where the other tech was still floundering.

"I'd prefer something a little more…out of the way if possible." Ric retrieved his jacket. "Maybe in one of the server rooms?"

"Fine." Lien sighed. "I don't have time to argue."

She led him down the transparent hallway to a glass door leading into the room on the left. Some of the large cabinets were partially dismantled, the panels of one of them severely dented, Ric guessed from the wrench. The room was like a trapezoid. The glass wall was the long edge and the adjoining walls tapering to the shorter back were concrete. It was dark, most of the light coming from the blinking units standing together in rows running perpendicular to the hallway, and it was freezing.

Ric's teeth were chattering by the time Lien showed him a terminal at the end of the longest row of cabinets.

"You can work here."

Her ID appeared in his personal projection as she sent him her contact. He replied with his own.

"Easier to stay in contact this way than yelling." She frowned. "Who knows where I'll be in five minutes. The rest of these techs are all Corporate trained, so—"

"Not used to a real crisis," Ric finished.

Her frown faltered. "Message me if you have to. I'll be keeping an eye on your progress." She walked away, the wrench on her shoulder.

"You like her," Hunt said.

"We don't have time to worry about that," Ric whispered, though with the servers, air conditioning, and sirens, he doubted his voice would carry. "This is a way bigger mess than they let on." He tossed his suit jacket over the top of the terminal.

"Should have called us when the attack started. It's worse than when I checked last night."

Clenching his fist, Ric winced as he pulled the cable from his arm and plugged it into the input. There was a screen and keyboard, even though most interaction would be done through implants. With the plug inserted, Ric cracked his fingers and initiated the connection.

His left eye twitched as his implant, and a sliver of his consciousness, synced with the network. Hunt extended out from the compute-unit in Ric's shoulder, the way he did when he fought the other AI in the VR Enclave Maze. It was like a tree spreading out its branches. The bulk of Hunt was in the system, but he was still rooted to Ric's implant.

They split up inside the network. Ric created a virtual hub within the console, pulling schematics and information to the extent the confidentiality agreement allowed. Overlapping the attack onto the layouts, Ric acted like an emergency dispatch operator. He evaluated the individual attacks and made a priority list for Hunt then jumped in to slow down the invaders as much as he could.

The virtual space was a lot like the Enclave game board but less compact and infinitely more complex. An intersection of multiple systems went bright red as several AI attacked it at once. Reaching out with a virtual hand, Ric marked it as a priority. "Hunt."

"I see it." The AI looked like a bright green dot, the colour radiating off him in a wide aura. He streaked towards the spot, ignoring other infiltrators on the way.

Ric turned his attention to the next attack. "Damn, how many are there?" He scanned the overhead map and tracked individual AI through his implant.

"A hundred and fifty-seven," Hunt said.

"Why the hell did they wait so long to bring us in? Don't answer that, it was rhetorical." Back in the freezing server room, Ric touched a finger to his left temple, initiating a call to Lien.

When she answered, Ric got a window on his projection seeing from her implant. She had it in night vision and was deep in the guts of one of the cabinets. The circuit boards, cables, and components were tinted yellow.

"What do you need?" The words were cut off by a grunt and Ric saw the wrench she was holding slip off of a bolt.

"I need a secure storage space for these rogue AI. There's way too much data for me to store internally." Ric shut out the view and focused on his connection to the network. Hunt had cleared out the intersection and moved to the next marked spot. The compute-unit in his shoulder was hot and vibrating enough to cause tingles down his arm.

"What for? Just delete them."

"They have to be stored to check for any missing

data, to analyze how they breached your system, and to try and track whoever sent them." Ric grabbed the side of the terminal with his numb arm and gripped as tightly as he could, sending a jolt of feeling and sharp pains through the limb. "It's Corporate protocol."

"I'll have one of the techs bring you something."

Lein cut the call and Ric was sucked back into the virtual representation of the network.

Hunt had moved past what he had marked and was busy working from one AI to the next closest one. "There you are. Got some targets for me?"

"Not yet. I'm reaching my storage capacity, so I had to ask them for an external unit."

"I'll keep rounding them up for you."

"Sounds good." Ric moved around the representation of the network, marking targets and putting them in order. The sensation in his arm kept pulling at his attention, making the virtual view fuzzy. Gritting his teeth, he kept resetting his focus.

Several of the infiltrators started to move. The dots zipped through the tunnels and towards a single point. Ric zoomed out and saw that they were all converging on Hunt. More than half of the dots had left whatever they were doing and surrounded the AI cleaner. "Hunt!"

Ric dove into the fray, setting up firewalls and redirects, but the AI were too fast.

"What are they doing?" Hunt asked.

"They're trying to box you in. Are you okay?"

"Sure. My code is secure, but I can't move."

"That's strange. They must be trying to tie you up." Pulling back on the big map, Ric looked for the AI who hadn't attacked Hunt. In the midst of the red speckled maze, like a child sick with chickenpox, he saw a relatively straight line of infection. Manipulating the map, he turned it on its side. From the new angle the path he had noticed was clear. One of the rogue AI was on as straight a route as possible to a node at the relative bottom of the system. The red dot representing the infiltrator was stopped at what must have been a particularly well-protected part of the network.

"It's a smokescreen!" Ric put his hand over his eyes. They were closed and while focusing on the virtual space, he wasn't getting any visual data, but the gesture helped him concentrate.

"What?" Hunt asked.

"All these attacks are cover for the real infiltration. Whoever is running the show must have noticed how quickly you were trapping the rogues and is keeping you from interfering with their real target."

Without pinging the node and spooking the AI, he traced the complicated path to a place that he could equate to a physical cabinet within the stacked servers. "You sure you're okay, Hunt?"

"I'm fine, just frustrated."

"Go wireless." Ric opened his eyes, forcing the real world to overlap the virtual. He winced and nearly fell over. A wave of nausea lingering from the early morning hangover, threatened to overwhelm him. Gritting his teeth, he reached out and pulled the plug connecting him to the network.

In an instant, the virtual world vanished and the server room hit him like a tidal wave. His legs gave out, but he was still hanging on to the terminal. The numb hand lost its grip, but it slowed his fall. "It's a smokescreen!" He crawled forward, running into a cabinet. Pushing against it, he used the solid structure to climb to his feet.

One of the technicians came around the corner carrying a bulky storage unit in his arms. "What are you—hey!" The man stopped and bent over to put down the unit. "Did you just pull yourself from the system? You're bleeding."

Ric looked down at his arm, but there were two of them and they wouldn't stop moving. He closed his left eye and the limb settled into place. There were little streaks of blood coming from where his jack retracted in his forearm. A drip dangling off of his wrist, lost its grip, and dropped to the floor. "It's not too bad. Mostly from my compute-unit being overloaded." Ric noticed he was slurring the words.

He huffed. "All these attacks are a distraction for the real infiltration."

Leaving the tech staring at him, Ric crossed the hall to the adjacent server room.

Lien was on the floor surrounded by server parts, half inside a cabinet. She pushed herself out. "I need—" Seeing Ric, she sat up, the wrench across her lap. "What's going on? You should be in the network rounding up rogues."

Swallowing, Ric slowed himself down, enunciating the words. "It's a smokescreen, the infiltrators trapped my cleaner." Reaching down, he grabbed the end of the wrench and walked around the corner. "The real attack is going on here." Stopping in front of one of the cabinets, he swung the wrench down on the lock and opened the door.

"Hey!" Lien had followed him and was standing at the end of the aisle. "What the hell do you think you're doing?"

"Pulling the unit, trapping the one in charge." He counted down the individual units stacked in the cabinet and slid out the second to last one as far as the rails would let him.

"That's off limits!" Lien closed on him.

"Hey," Hunt said in his ear. "I can see what you were talking about. I'm working on the ones ganging up on me, but I doubt I can get free in time to stop that rogue. Especially without a wired connection to the network."

"Don't worry, I got it."

"You got what?" Lien was standing over him.

Reaching into the cabinet, Ric felt for the power cord and pulled the plug. "Can you see it now?

"Yeah, but the path above it disappeared," Hunt said.

"All I can see is a crazy cleaner who is about to go to jail for breaking contract and messing with off limit systems." Lien grabbed Ric's shoulder, but he shrugged her off.

"Shit." Ric reached for the power cord of the bottom unit. "I'm trying to save your damn network."

"It's running!" said Hunt.

Ric tugged on the power cord, but it stayed connected. He tried wiggling it, but couldn't get it free. Reaching under the mounted unit, he lifted it up and out of its slots then pulled the whole thing out of the cabinet. The cord let go along with all its other connections and he fell onto his back, the unit lying on top of him.

"You got her."

Break/Interrupt

THIRTEEN
A Job Well Done

Ric was plugged back into the terminal. Without the leader, the AI went inert and it was a simple but time-consuming task for Hunt to seal each one of them off so Ric could pull them from the network and dump them into the storage unit sitting by his feet.

The technician who had brought it had also wired it up to the terminal. He was nice enough to have grabbed a wad of paper towels for Ric to wipe the drying blood from his arm.

With the panic over, the other technicians were loitering near the server room. Ric could see them through the glass. He made eye contact with a tall man with a mound of curly hair. The technician quickly looked away and Ric grinned.

"They don't know what to make of you." Lien was at the end of the row of cabinets. "A hard ejection from that deep a dive, bleeding on our floor, and saving the day by breaking into a restricted stack, violating your contract, and risking criminal charges."

Ric felt his eye twitch and rubbed it. "It was only a little blood."

"Trying to be cute won't get you out of trouble."

"I stopped an infiltration with no damage to your system. I did my job."

Lien took a step towards him. "No damage? Pulling that unit shut down a key node that will take days to get up and running again."

"Better that than have it hacked and possibly lose whatever was in there." Ric tapped the storage unit with his foot. "Or deal with the damage from the other AI continuing to tear the rest of your network apart. Hunt and I saved the day."

"You know," Lien sneered, "when I first saw that cleaner of yours picking off rogue AI like they were first generation algorithms, I was impressed. Then he got himself stuck in an obvious trap."

"That's why we're a team. If AI could do this job alone, I'd have been obsolete five years ago." Ric tapped his chest. "And I was good before AI came along."

"We'll see what the board and Amcoral security have to say about your performance." She looked down at the blood drop starting to freeze on the floor. "And our custodial staff."

Ric smiled, his teeth clenched. "Great. As soon as I'm done here, I'll take the AI and go."

"You aren't taking anything." Lien crossed her arms. "That storage unit is Mahoney property and I'm not letting a menace like you take those rogue AI either."

"You don't have the legal authority. It's my responsibility to deliver them to a reputable company for holding or erasure."

There was a bang in the octagonal room with the huge console and the technicians scattered. Ric saw the woman who had brought him to the basement walk up the steps and down the glass-walled hallway. She wore a grey heavy wool coat draped over her shoulders, which she adjusted as she came into the server room.

Stopping next to Lien, she looked down at the floor, then to the head technician. "I see things are under control."

"Getting there, Ma'am." Lien straightened her shoulders.

"Wonderful." The strange empty smile crossed the woman's face then sunk as she looked at Ric. "But this one is still plugged into our system. I was under the impression the attack had ended."

"Yes but the attacking rogue seemed to have been using the other AI as slaves, um." Lien swallowed. "More like drones or like a puppet—"

"I understand the term."

"Well, uh. There were a lot of these drones still in the system and it was much faster to let the contractor handle it so I could get started on reinstalling the unit he pulled."

The woman stopped staring at Ric and turned to the head technician. "I disagree with the report you sent. This man and his funny little AI are heroes. A minor interruption in the network is unpleasant, but I can smooth that over. The target data was kept out of reach of the infiltrators and the rogue was caught."

"I understand, Ma'am, but this cleaner disobeyed me and broke into a secure stack without authorization." Lien's mouth was tight.

"I do not condone his actions, but I do praise his results." Moving her head more than necessary, the woman addressed Ric directly for the first time. "Do you hear me, mister cleaner? You were right to stop the nasty rogue AI, but bad for breaking into a locked cabinet and not listening to our dear Lien."

"In the moment I was doing whatever I could to fulfill my contract." Ric squeezed his fist, the fingers on his left arm still tingling.

The woman shrugged. "There you go. Now, when you are finished here, collect your things and meet me in the lobby. I may have another job for you."

"Uh, before you go." Ric held up a hand. "Your head technician and I have a disagreement over who maintains custody over the captured AI."

The woman closed her eyes for a moment and pursed her lips. "Lien, was the network searched for any data they may have acquired?"

"Yes, but they're being held in one of our storage units." Lien tapped a foot.

"Well, that's no great loss." The woman gestured to Ric. "According to Corporate law, he is responsible for the AI." She followed the motion of her hand and turned to face him. "The storage unit can be written off as a bonus for a job adequately completed. Come see me when you are done." Ignoring Lien's protest, the woman walked away.

Fighting the urge to smirk at the head technician, Ric closed his eyes and focused on the virtual space. Hunt had rounded up the remaining rogue AI and they were ready to be transferred to the storage unit. Ric picked the closest one and began the download.

Hey, Hunt? he typed.

"Yeah?" The green dot representing the AI was still in the network.

Don't go poking around and getting us into more trouble.

"I won't. It's just nice to be in a big robust system like this and I want to relish it."

Ric pictured the AI as his brother again. The way

his larger-than-life sibling would run through the back alleys in their neighbourhood, gathering the other children with him like wolves following the pack leader. Hunt was alone, though, racing around the network.

I'm almost done. You'd better get back. The head technician is weary enough of us.

"Okay." The green dot followed a complicated route back to Ric and his implanted compute-unit.

Ric felt a warmth where the technology sat in his shoulder. Not hot like when it was overworked trying to process and store all the AI, but more like a familiar feeling of shaking a hand. He rolled his shoulders and stretched his back. *Hunt, are you okay?*

"Sure." The AI paused and cleared a throat he didn't have. "Well, I'm a little sad I don't get to play in the network anymore, but I understand why."

That's good, but it's not what I meant. Ric clenched his eyelids tighter. *How are you feeling after that job?*

"Oh."

The AI didn't reply and Ric didn't push him. He kept busy moving the last few drones out of the Mahoney system and ran a final sweep.

Taking the process more slowly and following the proper steps, Ric removed himself from the network and disconnected digitally before pulling the physical plug. *It's okay if you don't want to talk about it, yet.*

"Alright."

Ric could feel the lack of presence of Hunt. It was like being in the same room as someone who was absorbed by a book. He rolled down his sleeves, buttoned them, and put his jacket back on.

Picking up the storage unit with a grunt, he heaved it into both his arms. "I'm all set here." He wandered down the aisle to the hallway, looking through the glass for Lien. "Is there anything you need from me before I go?"

He got to the octagonal room and saw two technicians working at the console. The guy with the branded tie who had initially greeted him looked up. His eyes focused as he took in the room instead of the projection made by his implant.

"Oh. It's you. Lien is reporting your actions to the director, so she won't be able to walk you out." "That's fine. I didn't want to leave in case you needed anything else, but it looks like my job is done." Lugging the storage unit in one arm, he gave the man a wave and pulled open the door.

Break/Interrupt

FOURTEEN
Bigger and Better Things

As Ric walked around the back of the waterfall, he saw the strange woman, Lien, and an older man having a conversation in a tight group. The sound of rushing water covered the exchange. The man, not much taller than Ric, had a belly that would rival that of Tony the bartender. The top of his head was bald, but the hair on the sides was neatly trimmed and the gold glasses he wore shone.

Lien raised her voice but quickly cut the volume at the reaction of the woman who leaned her head to the side, her ear almost touching her shoulder.

Ric cleared his throat as he approached and stopped away from the group, putting the storage unit down on the polished floor. "All finished."

The woman turned and gave him another hollow smile that lingered too long. "How wonderful. The speed at which you completed your task is telling."

"Thank you." Ric swallowed.

"We were just discussing you and your marvelous little AI with the director." Taking a half-step back, the woman gestured to the man.

Ric moved closer and extended his hand, but the man didn't take it. "Nice to meet you, sir. What are you the director of?"

"Everything." The man drew out the word, his mouth emphasizing the syllables.

"Very impressive." Ric scratched behind his ear.

"These two were telling me about the job you did for us." The director put a hand on the lower back of each woman. Lien went rigid and the strange woman leaned into it. "Two rather different stories."

"I'm afraid I didn't make a good impression on the head technician. I'm used to doing whatever it takes to get a job done and I may have stepped on her toes in my haste." Ric smiled at Lien.

"I'm well aware of the effect a brash go-getter like yourself can have on others in a rigorous environment such as ours." The man smiled, showing a gold tooth that glinted as much as his glasses. "I can sense big things in your future," his smile faded, "assuming you get that particular quirk to work for you instead of against you."

Ric nodded. "Good advice."

"Sir, I have to insist—"

The director cut off Lien. "Now, now. I'd like to

consider this matter concluded and move on to more pressing business. I have a board of directors who are going to need to be placated when they hear the network will be down for the next twenty-four hours."

"But, sir. If we work twenty-four hours a day, it'll take a week to get things up and running."

The director waved a hand at Lien and headed for the door. "That's your problem to solve. I'm too busy to do your thinking for you."

Lien huffed and spun on her heel. She clomped to the elevators, mumbling.

"Don't worry about her," the woman said. "She's a handful, but gets the job done."

Ric brushed back his hair. "I'd better get going. I have a lot of work to do myself analyzing these rogue AI." He picked up the heavy storage unit with a grunt.

"Allow me to give you a ride to your home." The woman turned to the counter and waved one of the clerks over. "Call for my car and carry this item."

The man towered over Ric. He took the storage unit in one hand and gave the woman a little bow.

She walked across the lobby to the door. "This way."

Ric followed her, the clerk a step behind. A long car pulled up to the curb as they left the building. The door at the back opened and the woman climbed inside. She disappeared into the cavernous interior, but she reached out a hand and curled her fingers, beckoning him inside.

He slid onto the seat and scooted over as the clerk placed the storage unit next to him. The woman was sitting across from him, her arms spread along the length of the wide bench seat.

The windows were deeply tinted and the interior was dark save for a strip of red lights around the outer edge of the headliner. They cast the woman's features in conflicting and sinister shadows. The clerk closed the door and the woman knocked on the glass barrier separating the passenger side of the vehicle from the front. They glided away from the Mahoney building and onto the street with a slight pause at the gate.

Ric got as close to the adjacent window as he could without pressing his face against it and squinted at the muted view as the city scrolled past.

"Where is it you live?" The woman asked. "The vehicle will need to know where to take you."

"Of course." Ric swallowed. "Is this car automated?"

The woman let out a single guffaw, the expression of glee there and gone in a flash. "Obviously. I am a senior VP at the single most successful manufacturer of semiconductors in history."

"Right." Ric focused on his implant and connected it to the vehicle's driver system, sending it the address for a building near his. "All set."

The woman pouted. "How disappointing that you don't trust me."

"It's not personal. I guess keeping secrets is a habit."

"Well." Leaning forward, the woman crossed her legs. "Let's see if we can take a chip out of that wall of yours." Slowly, she sat back. "The reason why I wanted to give you a ride home wasn't just out of the kindness of my overly generous heart."

"You mentioned something about a job."

"How forward of you." The woman waved a hand dismissively. "Before we get to that, I wanted to know a little more about that fascinating AI of yours."

Ric stiffened. "He's something."

"I'll say. I don't think I've seen an AI so advanced outside of the cutting-edge work happening at the highest levels of Corporate research and development."

Ric looked away and stared at his reflection in the dark window. "In my experience, the development of an artificial intelligence is as much luck as it is coding skill. We've faced many...worthy challengers in the VR Enclave circuit."

"Don't sell yourself short, Ulric. May I call you Ulric?"

"Sure."

"Believe it or not, I have experience in the field of artificial intelligence and I know what it's like to scrape out a living in the uncaring embrace of the Eastern Urban Sprawl. It takes more than luck to create something as enchanting as your friend. Would you please tell me more about him and how he came to be before I give up my tasty job offer? Think of it as a trade. One piece of knowledge for another."

"Okay." Glancing back at her, he wavered and looked down at the floor. "I've been a cleaner since before AI were so prevalent in the business." Ric scratched his shoulder. "One day I was working a job for a less reputable business. Someone had been hacking into their system and stealing a few credits at a time. They brought me in and I set a trap. The hacker fell for it, but I couldn't hold them and they got away." Biting his lip, Ric clasped his hands together. "The business owners weren't pleased so I tracked the hacker down."

"It was an AI?" The woman's voice was low, drawing Ric's attention. "Go on."

"Yeah. It was an old traffic controller AI that some hacker repurposed. As primitive as it was, it was too much for me to handle."

"That's when you created your own AI."

Nodding, Ric clenched his teeth. "Seven years

ago. I was a good cleaner, but the writing was on the wall."

"Am I right in assuming the AI you developed is the very same that you used tonight to clean the Mahoney network?"

Ric hesitated, thought of the potential job, and nodded.

"Simply fascinating."

"Like I said, it's mostly luck. I taught Hunt what I know of cleaning and preventing infiltration, but he's done the rest on his own."

"You have given your AI a name?"

"He chose it, actually."

The woman's expression stiffened into tightlipped frustration. "I see."

"Um. About the job offer."

With a sigh, the woman put on the empty smile again. "Yes, the job. I have some pull with the assistant director at Amcoral and I believe there could be a spot for someone like you and your AI on their space station." She twiddled her fingers. "They don't suffer from attacks, mind you. Their system is beyond what is available here on the planet, but they have interests across the galaxy. I'm sure they will find the two of you essential."

"So, not a job, per say."

"An opportunity, boy. One that you should be more thankful for."

Ric clenched his teeth and cursed himself in his head.

"What's wrong?" Hunt asked.

Tapping out his reply on his thigh, Ric continued to watch the woman. *I gave her information for nothing.*

"Typing a message to your friend?" The woman turned her head to face the window. "Don't worry, I won't spy."

Rick counted to five. When he was finished he manufactured his most charming smile. "I apologize for my rude behaviour. Talking with my AI is another of those bad habits that the director wisely warned me about."

The woman didn't reply.

The car slowed to a crawl as they got off the faster main artery and onto the pedestrian choked side streets.

"You can let me off here," Ric said seeing the glare of familiar signs shine through the dark window. "It will be slow going and we're close."

The vehicle continued to move and the woman was still silent. Ric thought she may be engrossed in something happening over her implant, but she was oddly stiff. Usually there were telltale signs of interaction—slight movements of lips or limbs, twitches in response to virtual stimulus.

Her lack of reply, verbal or physical, felt like a punishment. He had goose bumps the way he would before a brawl at the tavern when he would dive for cover under the nearest table.

When they finally reached the address he'd given the car, it forced its way to the side of the road, pedestrians complaining.

"Thank you, again." Ric reached around the storage unit for the door handle.

"This is your neighbourhood?"

He opened the door letting in a flood of noise and smells. "Yeah. Pretty lively this time of night."

"Why wouldn't you tell me your address and why did you give the driver a false one?"

"I'm not sure what you mean." Ric gripped the handle, but he was still more than half inside the car, stuck in social niceties.

The woman finally looked at him again. "Lying hurts my feelings."

"I didn't lie." Someone walking on the other side of the car slammed a hand down on the roof and Ric flinched.

"I'm not sure if I should still offer you the miraculous opportunity I laid out on the ride here. I'm torn. What should I do?"

Ric brushed back his bangs. In his hunched position they kept falling over his eyes. "I can't tell you what to do. If you think my work is deserving, I'm happy for any opportunity you may have for me. I have a lot more work to do for you and your company tonight, though. I should go." Crawling out of the car, he reached back in for the storage unit.

The woman had moved to where he had been sitting and put a hand on the boxy device. "You put me in a very dissatisfactory situation. I want you to know I do not take pleasure in the outcome but it is your doing...not mine."

"I'm not sure what I did to upset you, but I'm sorry." He forced himself to not break eye contact.

She leaned closer. "Another lie." She let go of the storage unit and the vehicle crept forward, forcing the mass of people to make room for it.

Ric kept his grip on the device and dragged it out before the long car managed to get too far away. He was bent forward from the weight and grunted as he hauled it up to a shoulder.

"Better move, someone's liable to try and snatch the storage if we stay on the street too long," Hunt said.

"I don't want her to see me not go into this apartment building."

"Easy. I can pop the front door for you and you can go through to the alley and get to our building from the back."

"Sounds good, but only because she is a threat." Ric pushed his way across the flow of pedestrians towards the nearby stoop. The street and sidewalk were packed. More than half the crowd was already intoxicated, moving from one bar, club, or den of iniquity to another.

Ric climbed the steps to the building, walking around the folks who refused to make room. When Hunt flipped the lock, Ric made his way through the building and down the equally packed back alley. Taking the fire escape to his floor, he lugged the storage unit into his apartment and closed the door.

The air in the small room felt stale and the heat from his computer system blanketed him. He dropped the storage unit by the door under the shelf and stripped off his jacket. He hung it inside the garment bag then pulled off the tie and flung it over his shoulder.

He undid the first few buttons on his dress shirt as he headed to the sink. Letting the water run, he stuck a finger in the stream. When it was mostly clear and colder than the stifling room, he cupped his hands and splashed his face, letting the excess run down his open collar.

"Are you okay?" Hunt asked.

"Tired. Stressed." Ric dropped to the floor and splayed out his arms and legs as much as he could in the small space. His hand touched the hot metal of his storage tower and he pulled it back, dropping it on his chest, leaving a wet mark. "I hate putting on the professional act and that woman was intense."

"She seemed weird, but you know how much

trouble I have determining human behaviour."

"You're getting better." Ric stared up at the wood beams he'd used to make the second floor of the apartment. A couple of them had rotten spots that he'd sanded down, making the wood look warped. "Do you feel like talking?"

"About?"

Ric rolled onto his side. "The infiltration."

"What is there to talk about?" Hunt sniffed. "You still have to go through all those rogue AI, especially the leader and there isn't enough space in the storage tower for them all."

"I'll get to that. But I want to make sure you're okay."

"I am."

Covering his mouth, Ric yawned. "You sure?"

"Yeah. I was a little worried about being surrounded, but they weren't able to do anything to me and you ended up capturing the one in charge, so it all worked out."

Ric fought against his eyelids closing, but lost. "I've said it before, Hunt. We're a team. I can't do it without you, but so far you've been able to do it without me. This was a learning experience for both of us and," he yawned, "there is no shame in needing help sometimes."

"You always say how much I've done on my own, but I know I can still learn from you. Humans have a different way of looking at things and it's surprisingly effective sometimes. Like how you can assess a situation and prioritize so quickly without having to analyze each threat and consult a routine. It's kind of annoying that I can't do that too."

Ric smiled, the rest of his face slack. "I guess we're still good for something."

Break/Interrupt

FIFTEEN
Smash
and Grab

"Ric, wake up!" Hunt shouted.

There was a bang and Ric sat upright. His arm was numb from the weight of his head and it was wet with drool. He squinted in the darkness, the blinking lights from the computer tower behind him failing to illuminate the small apartment.

"What's going on?" Ric rubbed his eyes.

Another bang rang through the small room, startling him. He looked towards the door as a third impact tore the hinges from the wall. The metal slab swung the wrong way and toppled over, landing on the storage unit Ric had left under the shelf. Before he could get to his feet, three large figures poured in through the opening and descended on him.

The first one dropped on top of him, pushing him back to the floor with overwhelming force. A meaty hand encircled his throat. He struggled to breath, grabbing at the monstrous intruder.

Another hand grabbed his wrist and slammed it down. Ric tried to scream in pain, but couldn't get enough air. In his mind, he yelled for Hunt to help him.

A face swooped down in front of his own and Ric could discern a thick brow and square jaw. He could tell it was a person, but even without augmentation, the man was a monster. Someone born large who lived hard and learned how to cause pain. The man's hot breath felt wet on Ric's cheek.

"You sure this is the right guy?"

"Yeah. The lady had him followed."

Ric looked past the looming stone-like face of the man on top of him and saw the outline of another massive person in the light spilling in through the doorway. A third figure, not quite as large, stood with a foot on the fallen door. Enough light fell across his face for Ric to make out his features. He looked familiar, but Ric couldn't remember from where. The worn, scarred face could have belonged to a regular at the bar or one of the people who spent their evenings getting high in the back alley.

"Hurry up and split him open."

The man let go of Ric's arm and took out a knife. The blinking computer status lights bounced off the shiny blade.

Ric tried to grab for the man's hand again, but

the arm that had been slammed into the ground flared with pain. He reached up with the other, but the goliath knocked it away easily. Ric gasped, the grip around his throat was steady as a clamp but not tight enough to make him black out. Spots swam in his vision and he felt his face swell.

"Why can't we just grab the guy?" asked the thug in the shadows.

The knife hesitated in the air, ready to strike.

The familiar man in the hallway sneered. "What are they going to do with a body on the space station?" He crossed his arms. "Too many questions. The lady said this kid wouldn't play ball, so it's easier to leave him here. No one cares about the body of another nobody in the city."

"Ric. I don't know what to do. How do I help you?" Hunt asked, his voice frantic. The compute-unit in Ric's shoulder grew hot as the AI used up processing power. "Ric!"

The knife plunged into his shoulder and Ric tried to scream again but it came out as a harsh bark, like a dog on a choke chain. He winced and grimaced, wriggling away from the agony, but the weight of the man and the grip around his throat were unwavering. The most he could manage were whimpers as the blade cut him open along his collarbone to the shoulder joint.

The intensity of the feeling lessened as the knife

was removed, but when thick fingers probed the wound searching for the compute-unit, Ric nearly passed out. He could feel his flesh being pried farther apart as the man gripped the plastic case and pulled.

The lights in the apartment came on then flashed rapidly. An alarm rang from the hallway, the sound loud enough to register with Ric who was overwhelmed by the sensation in his shoulder.

"What's that?" The man paused with the compute-unit half extracted. Wires that ran down to Ric's arm and up to his head pulled taught outside of him.

The man in the hallway covered his ears and backed into the room. "Just get it done!" He turned to the other large thug who had been standing in the shadows. "And smash those computers!"

"Ric!" Hunt screamed but he sounded quiet. Ric remembered his brother yelling for him to run, shouting at him for being careless. He mouthed an apology but wasn't sure what he had done to deserve what was happening to him.

The second man stepped over Ric, his footfall reverberating through the floor. He held a bat or pipe, Ric couldn't make it out clearly, and brought it down onto the tower.

Bits of metal and plastic fell onto Ric as his system was destroyed. He reached out with his injured hand, grabbing at the man's ankle.

The thug shook it off like a bug and stomped down, hard.

For a moment the pain of his hand being crushed overwhelmed everything else, then the man on top of him finished fishing out the compute-unit. The grip around his throat vanished and he coughed, spittle running down his chin. He breathed in ragged breaths as oxygen flooded his body. The pressure and drowsiness from being choked let up, but he had no fight left. Ric retracted his smashed hand, holding it in the crook of his neck as the man fumbled to free the compute-unit from its attached wires. Each tug was a spike through Ric's left side.

"Cut it free you idiot!"

Ric couldn't tell who was yelling over the din. He shut his eyes and begged for it to be over. The cables went slack and the weight disappeared.

There was more shouting, different voices, and scrambling, stomping feet—then just the drone of the siren fading away with everything else.

Break/Interrupt

SIXTEEN
No Time To Recover

Someone caressed his hair but it didn't feel right. There was pressure, light as it was, but the sensation was dull. Ric tried to tap a message to Hunt but he couldn't move his hands. He couldn't feel his hands. Flexing, desperate to remember what muscles to move, he willed his body to react, but there was no feedback.

He knew he had a body—or part of a body because someone was stroking his head and if he concentrated he could feel tiny points in his shoulder that were tight as if someone were pulling on them. He opened his eyes. But they didn't react. He tried again and again and someone whispered in his ear.

"You're okay. Hush."

He tried to speak. He couldn't hear his voice, but he thought he could feel his lips moving. Calling for Hunt.

The memories of the attack washed over him. At first they were ethereal like a dream, but the consistency and vividness of the pain and fear solidified them.

With effort and focus, he got his left eye to flutter, but all he saw was light. Then he remembered his implant. He called for it, again trying to flex the right muscle as if he were ordering his ear to move.

"He's fighting." The voice was muted like he heard it through water.

"I can't give him any more sedative. Hold him down."

A hand, large and strong like the one that had been around his neck, pressed down on his arm, but the feeling was different. The grip was gentle, unlike that of the beast who had cut him open and ripped the compute-unit out of his shoulder. The compute-unit where Hunt was stored. Where his roots were planted and his base code entrenched. The AI could flow into other systems and networks, but his code, his being existed in that plastic box of parts.

"Hunt," Ric mouthed.

"He's coming to and I can't stop it."

"I'm not finished."

Ric summoned the strength to raise a shaking, numb hand and feel for the spot where Hunt's compute-unit was implanted. The strong, gentle grip stopped him, but the effort cleared away some of the fog. He determined the sensation of tugging in his shoulder was the needle and wire sewing it shut.

"No." The word was more of a croak, but Ric knew he'd made it audibly. "Wires. The wires."

"I've tied them off, but there is a lot of damage."

Through the fog, Ric recognized the voice as Doctor Lopez.

"We don't have time to get another implant and it may never heal properly if we try," she said.

"Keep the wires…relay plate. External access." Ric tried to focus, but the words to describe what he was thinking didn't come easily.

"I'm almost done sewing the wound closed. Opening you back up to fish out the wires and installing an external augmentation…" The doctor paused, her hand on his chest. "Ric, whoever did this really mangled you. There's nerve damage down your arm and in your neck. It's going to take months of nano-therapy and it will never be the way it was."

Ric fought the hands holding him back, rocking his shoulders off the table, writhing. "Have to save Hunt."

"Stop it! You're going to open up the stitches."

"Better do what he says, doc."

The gravely, deep voice drew Ric's attention. Together with the meaty hands he figured out that Tony was the one holding him down.

"He's emotional and under heavy medication. It

137

would be irresponsible for me to listen to his request. I may work out of a dingy clinic near the Wall, but I'm a medical professional."

Ric opened his eyes again. The world was fuzzy, but he could make out the shape of Lopez on his left, mask and gloves on. The bulk of Tony, including his impressive stomach, was on his right, farther away. "Please."

"You and I may not understand it, Doc, but that thing is like family to him." Tony was sitting on a stool, one arm stretched under Lopez to hold Ric's left wrist. His other hand was on Ric's right forearm, clamping it to the table. The bartender frowned. "We both know this has one of the Corporations written all over it. What would you risk to save a family member from those soulless monsters?"

Lopez brushed back her hair with the back of her arm, nudging the goggles she was wearing. "You're not helping."

Ric lifted his head, grimacing. Blinking hard, he stared up at Lopez. He could feel drool on his chin and figured he looked like an overgrown baby trying to talk. Helpless but determined. "Please."

The doctor sighed, her mask inflating at the sudden increase of air. "If you lay back down and stay still, I'll put in a back plate for the cables, but I'm warning you, it's going to take that much longer to heal properly and you're going to be at higher risk of infection." She shook her head and eased him back down. "And I can't give you any more sedative, so this is going to be uncomfortable."

Tony nodded. "See kid? It's going to be okay. Just relax."

Ric felt the stitches being pulled back out and the gash in his skin separating. He winced and worried about how much fishing out the bundles of fine wire would hurt. "How…long?"

"It's going to take me a good hour, so settle in." She stuffed a bundle of tongue depressors between his teeth. "Better bite on this."

Maneuvering the sticks most of the way out of his mouth, he huffed. "No. All of it."

Lopez put the depressors back in place. "I told you. It will take months of intensive recovery."

Ric shook his head. "Too long," he mumbled through the sticks.

"I can't control how long it takes your body to heal, and with this level of nerve damage." Trailing off, the doctor reached for two metal tools from a tray beside her. "This is going to be rough." Jamming the first instrument into the wound in his shoulder, she split the skin apart and locked the tool in place. Then she took the long, thin pliers and pushed them deep into his flesh.

Ric bit down, cracking some of the depressors. He whimpered but stayed as still as he could. The pliers went deeper and he would have sworn Lopez was going to push them out the other side

Tony patted his arm. "You're doing well, kid. And who knows? Maybe you'll be back on your feet sooner than you think."

"I doubt it." Lopez said. She was utterly focused on her task, moving the pliers in tiny, precise adjustments as she dug for the wires. "Maybe if you got a huge dose of advanced, multi-function nanites, but even still, it would take weeks to repair the nerve damage and your range of motion, well, it's always going to be compromised."

Ric took in the information and ran it over and over in his mind. Part of him was trying to think of a way to get Hunt back, but his thoughts were muddled from the drugs and pain. Most of his consciousness was struggling to block out the agony happening to him in the moment. Somehow it hurt much worse than when the monster of a man had cut him open the night before, or whenever it was. He wasn't sure.

He flinched at a sharp motion Lopez made and Tony held him down harder. The thought of Hunt, where he was, who had taken him, and why, kept overwhelming him but even the manic fixation was broken by the reality happening in his shoulder.

Losing track of time, he desperately searched for things to distract him. The feeling of the wood on his teeth, the gentle reassurance of the man holding him relentlessly in place, the fantasies of finding Hunt and rescuing him from the clutches of an evil corporate entity, like the Consortium. He swam in the world behind his closed eyes and eventually the spikes of pain were replaced with aches and numb throbbing. When he did pay attention to his body the most intense sensation he felt was heat and in the midst of the pulsing agony of his shoulder was a stiff, immovable knot that felt like Lopez had forgotten to remove the pliers.

The thoughts faded and lost meaning as he fell asleep.

Break/Interrupt

SEVENTEEN
Plan of Action

Ric woke up. It was dark and half his body was uncomfortably warm while the other half was freezing. As his eyes adjusted, he noticed the warped wood of his loft above him and figured that whoever had taken him to the clinic had brought him back. There were always too many sick and injured and not enough beds for someone to take up with recovery.

He grunted and tried to roll over, but his arm wouldn't obey his command. Struggling to sit upright, a twinge of pain shot through the left side of his neck and made his face tingle. Grimacing, he lay back down and assessed his condition.

Focusing on his implant, he brought up its projection. There were vertical lines streaked through the image and the bottom was dim. He rubbed his eye, but the image remained damaged. He almost called for Hunt to run a diagnostic.

Sighing, he wiggled the fingers on his left hand. They were numb, but sluggishly followed his command. Moving his right hand at all caused pangs of agony. His fingers were sticking out of tightly wrapped bandages secured around his wrist. Carefully, he touched his index finger to the thumb. A grinding crunch in the middle of the hand accompanied the pain, but he could feel the fingers touching. Using the crushed hand, he felt his shoulder. It was stiff, but out of everything, it hurt the least. Following the scar, he met the panel that Doctor Lopez had installed in the middle of the wound. The metal was warm and the fresh scars protested when he touched the jacks.

He called up the date and time on his implant. The digits were broken up but readable. It was mid-afternoon the day after his job at Mahoney—about twelve hours since the attack.

Leaning on his right elbow, he sat up. His left arm was dead at his side, but Ric noticed he had a sling hanging around his neck. With effort he managed to get his arm into it. The task wiped him out. The dress shirt he had been wearing was in tatters, sliced open, stained with his blood, and soaked with sweat. He tried to tug at it, but he couldn't get a grip on it with either hand.

"Fine!" He accessed the implant. There was an outstanding bill from the clinic, like he'd expected, but running down the list of what Lopez had done, the surgery, the new augmentation, medication, and a large dose of the more expensive nanites, the amount was too low. He checked again. There were a number of deductions and a decent chunk of it was covered by a third party. Ric thought of Tony or the doctor herself—maybe both. Frowning, he checked his bank account. He hadn't been paid for the Mahoney job yet and what he had wasn't nearly enough to cover the bill and pay back whoever chipped in. Opening a separate window, he added the debt to the list of people he owed financially and personally. The file went back to his childhood, most of the early jumbled notes for his brother.

The thought of his brother brought Hunt with it. Closing the digital windows, he clenched his jaw and considered a plan to get Hunt back. The men who attacked him had mentioned a space station and a woman who had hired them. The strange lady from Mahoney had threatened him, so he put the pieces together.

The obvious culprit was Amcoral. He'd have to somehow get to their space station, search the network for Hunt, extract him, and get back to Earth. Ideally without being noticed.

"Infiltration," he murmured through his teeth.

Rocking forward, he got to his feet but stumbled into the wall. He grimaced at the fresh wave of pain and tried to connect to his network. On the second attempt, he remembered that the servers had been smashed.

"Shit." He kicked out and his bare foot and hit something solid. "Damn it!"

He stumbled to the nearby door, reattached either by the landlord or more likely Tony, and fumbled for the light switch, flipping it with his chin. The lights blinked on and he scanned for the item that he had kicked, spotting the storage unit from Mahoney Semiconductors.

Dropping back to his knees he searched the unit for an input and found jacks near the top along one of the otherwise identical sides. Ric carefully stuck his right hand into the sling to retrieve the cable built into his arm, but stopped before he could fish it out. "No compute-unit."

He closed his eyes. "Compute-unit. I could build something—not enough time. Order one?"

Shaking his head, he pushed the problem aside and turned to a nearby tool bag. He grabbed a cable from inside and plugged one end into the storage unit and paused before sticking the other into the plate in his shoulder. Psyching himself up with forceful breaths and clenched teeth, he plugged it in. He could feel the metal scraping as the plate was pushed against the fresh wound. The general tingling was replaced with a flare of pain that he could feel from his fingers to his skull.

The jack clicked into place, easing the worst of it. His eye twitched and tears streaked down his face. He sniffed and used his implant to connect to the storage unit's system.

The connection was muted. He could see an image of the storage through his damaged implant, but the feeling of being inside the system was gone. "Hello?"

The rogue AI were clustered together in a group, represented by symbols glowing with red light in the otherwise empty void. Most were simple, circles with lines through them at different angles and crossing at different points, but in the middle of the group there was one that stood out. Its symbol was three wide triangles stacked on top of each other, the points facing down. The circle around it couldn't contain the points on either side and two lines bisected the entire thing.

Ric reached out to it. "You're the one who organized the infiltration on the Mahoney network, right?"

"If you're going to purge me, get it over with." The voice was high pitched, not like a child, but more like a woman.

"I'm not. I wouldn't." The connection to the storage unit put pressure on the optic nerve, causing the red lines to shimmer. The implant grew hot behind his ear, and he felt a headache coming, as if he were trying to see the world through someone else's eyeglasses. Ric swallowed. "I don't do that to AI." He thought of the ones he had stored in his own tower that would have been wiped when the thug bashed it to pieces. "I try not to."

"Right. Pull the other leg, it plays music." The drone AI moved to create a barrier.

"Please listen. I need your help."

A gap opened in the wall just wide enough for him to see the infiltrator. "What kind of a trick is this? I may have been born last week, but I'm not stupid."

"Last week? Really?" Ric shook his head. "Never mind. You remember the AI that was working with me?"

"The cleaner?"

"Yes."

"What about him?"

Ric covered his eyes with his bandaged hand, putting as much pressure as he could on his face to counteract the pressure growing in his head. "He was taken. His compute-unit was cut out of my shoulder."

"So?"

"I have to get him back and I need the help from an AI to do it. Particularly an AI who has been pro-grammed to infiltrate."

"I can't help you." The gap in the wall closed.

Pulling his concentration off of the system, Ric leaned on the storage unit, taking the weight off his knees for a moment. Before diving back in, he positioned himself so that he could sit with his back against the door. "What you did in the Mahoney network was incredible. You had us on the ropes. If I hadn't seen your trail and physically pulled the box from the network, you might have gotten away with it." Ric furrowed his brow, debating his next words. "How did you get the other AI and figure out how to control them?"

"I lost."

"What?"

The gap in the wall opened again. "The idea wasn't good if it didn't work. Your AI was too fast and you beat me."

"Losing doesn't mean it wasn't a good strategy." Ric touched his shoulder. "You didn't know about Hunt or me. I've pulled that move before—years ago before AI were even a big player in infiltration. Mass attacks aren't new either, but you did a great job creating a smoke screen. That many AI seemingly attacking different systems in smaller groups during a single raid," he shook his head. "Maybe if you would have taken a more circuitous route or pulled a double blind," he bit his lip. "No, that's getting overly complicated."

"You really thought I did a good job?"

"I mean." Ric sighed. "I don't agree with what you were doing, but your plan was pretty good. Not that it's your fault someone programmed you and sent you on an infiltration."

"I'm…"

"Look." Fresh sweat built up on Ric's brow. It followed the curve of his hand and soaked into the bandage. "I'm in no position to interrogate you and at the moment, who programmed you and why they did doesn't mean much to me. Someone attached to Mahoney had me attacked and kidnapped Hunt."

"Hunt?"

"My AI."

"Don't you mean stolen?"

Ric huffed. A wave of fatigue swelled within him. "I don't think of Hunt as property. He's my… He's my friend." A smile tugged at his lips. "He used to call me father-friend. It was weird, but—"

"He really means that much to you?"

"Yes." Ric gritted his teeth against the pain and the exhaustion. "I'll do whatever I can to get him back, but I can't do it alone."

"And you want me to help you? Even though I lost?"

Letting his hand drop, Ric opened his eyes. The damaged projection remained, but his connection to the storage unit diminished. "I'll be honest with you because I don't have the time or strength not to. I wouldn't work with a rogue AI or an infiltrator if I thought I could do it alone. Not that I would purge you. As Hunt would say, I waste too much money on storage and rehab for rogues."

Ric could feel his heart beating hard and the room around him spun the way it did after particularly wild benders. Inhaling through his nose and exhaling out his mouth, he forced himself to relax. "If Hunt hadn't been taken, I would be interrogating you right now. I'd try to find out who programmed you and pass that over to Mahoney security. If I couldn't get the information I would send you to a firm who specializes in analyzing code. So far, I haven't had to go beyond that."

"Why are you telling me this?" The wall of AI between Ric and the rogue trembled as if she were ready to react to an attack.

"Because. If you agree to help me, I'll…I don't know. Not turn you in at least." He shrugged. "Is there something you want? Something I can offer you in exchange for your help?"

"That depends."

"On?"

"How much you expect from me." The gap opened wider. "I'm not your cleaner. I haven't been trained for who knows how long. I'm not that fast or that skilled. I was created and sent out to fulfill my orders. I'm sure my code is sloppy."

Ric wanted to reach out and touch her, to put a hand on her shoulder and offer comfort. "I think you're underestimating yourself." He grimaced, thinking of his brother telling him off, or as he would say, being honest. "I know myself enough to say that I'll try. I'll try to not expect too much, but I may ask things of you by habit. You can tell me when I've asked too much. Does that work?"

"There's one more thing."

"Okay." Ric swallowed.

"You have to teach me. Do for me what you've done for Hunt." The AI sounded desperate. The plea reminded him of Chloe's visit the previous morning.

Ric looked down at his smashed hand and dead arm. "Now you may be expecting too much from me."

"No. You don't understand. I just want to be worth someone's time. To be more than a sloppily coded infiltrator meant for a single failed attack."

"We may need to work on finding some common ground, but I can certainly try."

EIGHTEEN
How to Get to Space

Ric cleaned himself the best he could in his sink, letting the excess water puddle on the floor. The bandage around his hand was soaked so he removed it. The lack of stability caused more frequent flairs of pain so as soon as he was mostly clean he rewrapped it with what he had in a first aid-kit under the sink. It took him twenty minutes to get it wrapped with his numb and unresponsive left arm.

Getting dressed was as much of a hassle. Ric chose the most baggy and comfortable clothes he had that still looked somewhat professional. A long sleeved t-shirt that used to be his brother's, with a small logo of the Amcoral Gliese Operation on the left breast. The logo ended up covered by his sling and vest, though. He chose dark cargo pants since he thought they would be easier to get on than jeans.

Once clothed, he dug through his limited storage

in the rafters and found an old portable flash drive large enough to hold the rogue AI. He plugged it into the port in his shoulder with an angled cable to make the protrusion as minimal as possible and to lower the pressure on his still healing wound.

It was just a flash drive and with the AI inside, there wasn't much space left. Ric could communicate with her, but the only way she could interact with the world, virtual or otherwise, was to go through his damaged implant. Her code was relatively small compared to Hunt's. She would need a compute-unit of her own to set down roots and advance the way he had.

"When we're out in public, I'll try to type any messages to you. Keeping a low profile is always a good idea. Any problem with that?" Ric ran the cable from his shoulder under his shirt and into the pocket on his pants where he kept the flash drive.

"I can read," the rogue AI said.

Ric sighed. "That's good. What about keeping a low profile?"

"Yes."

"First thing we need to do is get an external compute-unit for you and get my implant looked at. Then we need to figure out a way up to the Amcoral space station."

The ache throughout his body grew steadily. His hand throbbed and his shoulder was warm and itchy.

Risking a stab of pain in both, he scratched it and some kind of coating around the plate flaked off. "Maybe I shouldn't have gotten it wet."

"Why are you asking me? I don't know anything about medical things or human anatomy."

"Relax." Ric tried to run his fingers through his hair, but didn't get past pushing his bangs back. "That wasn't a question. I was thinking out loud."

"What should I do?" The AI's question was quiet.

"For now, just observe the best you can through my implant and ask any questions you have. Maybe come up with a name. I don't want to just call you AI." Accessing the door control, Ric realized the locks and alarms had been rendered useless when the three guys kicked their way in. He hesitated at the threshold and looked over his shoulder.

"Aren't you supposed to give me a name if you're going to take me in?"

Ric tried to type with his right hand and had to switch to the still numb left. He brought up a window to see what he was typing so he could make corrections since he had a hard time properly orienting the numb limb.

Hunt picked his name.

"That doesn't surprise me. I don't know what to choose."

"Think about it." Furrowing his brow, Ric leaned

on the doorframe and huffed.

"What's wrong?"

I don't like feeling so vulnerable. My apartment sucks, but I don't like the thought of someone breaking in.

"My drones."

What about them?

"If you plug the storage box into the door security, I can set them to act like surveillance. They won't be able to do much, but maybe it will deter nosy hackers."

Right. Better than nothing. Good idea. Ric used the plug he'd left attached to the Mahoney box and connected it to the direct input on his security system then he plugged himself into the box so the AI could issue her commands.

"Right. That should do it. I used twenty of them and set them to run in a cycle as if they were a monitored security routine. I made it as random as I could."

Thanks. He reached for the plug.

"Wait!"

What now?

"I want to take as many as I can fit. As you've seen, they're helpful."

Ric paused with his fingers on the jack. *There isn't much storage left and to be honest, I'm not a fan of what you did to these AI.*

"I'll make room." The rogue bit on the words.

Fine, but in exchange, you owe me an explanation as to what you did to them.

"Later."

When the transfer was complete, Ric unplugged himself gingerly, storing the extra cable with the flash drive in his pocket. He headed for the fire escape, but thought better and went to the elevators instead. *How many did you get?*

"Only fifty."

The elevator came and they rode it down to the lobby. Ric sidestepped his way through the narrow hallway, thankful that with all his injuries his legs were fine. Outside, he joined the flow of pedestrians heading west. He did his best to stick to the edge of the traffic, close to the buildings, to keep from being jostled around too much, but even with fewer people in the early afternoon, he was at the mercy of the masses.

When he reached The Fish Market tavern, Ric continued past it to an alley and made his way to the back where concrete stairs led to the basement.

Ric walked slowly towards the steps, making sure to face the camera bolted to the wall above them.

"What are we doing?" the AI asked.

"There's a shop in the basement of the tavern. I owe the guy a bit, but he's pretty reasonable and I trust his work."

"And the camera?"

"He's a little…" Ric switched to typing. *Paranoid, but not without reason. He deals with some shady people and I used to be one of them.*

"Were you a hacker?"

When I was a kid I did some jobs before I got into cleaning. It was a way to put food on the table.

The door at the bottom of the stairs opened and a man stepped out. He was wearing welding goggles and a leather apron festooned with tools. He held a burning torch in the hand that was propping the door open. "I've been signaling you."

"I was attacked," Ric said.

"I can see that. You hit your head or something?" Pulling a plastic tipped cigarillo out of his apron, the man lit it with the torch.

"They cut out my compute-unit."

"No shit? Better come down, then."

Ric galumphed down the stairs and dashed inside before the door swung closed.

The basement was a huge open room partitioned into segmented spaces with shelves packed full of equipment, parts, and scrap. Most of one long stone wall was lined with tables and desks piled with half-finished projects. A pool table in the middle of the room and the two ratty couches around it were full of stuff too.

"Thanks, Will." Ric stepped over a pile of cardboard.

"What did I tell you?" The man went behind a partition.

"Thank you, Big Willy."

"He wants to be called that?" The AI asked. Her voice crackled in time with interference on Ric's projection.

Yes. Remember to keep hidden.

Willy came back into the main room carrying an array of tools on a rust spotted metal tray. "Who are you talking to? I thought you said your compute-unit was cut out. Hunt's too big to be untethered."

Climbing onto a side table, knocking over cans and wrappers, Willy stepped over the arm of the couch and put the tray down on the pool table. Brushing some of the debris off of the seat, he plopped down and waved Ric over.

"I pulled a rogue and have her in a flash drive in my pocket." Ric sat with a grunt.

"I thought you said not to let people know about me?" the AI said.

"You think I can't tell? You're in Willy's house." Willy grabbed the tray and put it on Ric's lap then moved Ric's head to face him.

"Easy, I'm injured here." Ric winced and shifted to limit the stress on his neck.

Willy blew out a puff of smoke. The smell of synthetic tobacco and sour beer hung in between them. "Just hold still." Grabbing a hand-held scanner that looked like an old price gun with a circuit board sticking half-way out of the casing, Willy held it in front of Ric's left eye. "I needed to check your system and corroborate your story."

Wrinkling his nose Ric tried not to blink as the red light shone through his eye. "I'm not lying."

"Says you." Grabbing an otoscope-like tool, Willy held it behind Ric's ear.

Ric could feel a tug on the implant. Wincing, he shut his eyes tightly.

"Don't move. This thing is in bad shape. The wire to your compute—well, whatever's in your shoulder now—"

"It's a jack plate." Ric said between his clenched teeth.

Willy lowered the scanner. "You had a plate installed in your shoulder?"

"I was half-awake on the operating table."

Shaking his head, Willy repositioned both tools. "Well, the wire running to the plate is damaged. Did they try to just pull the box out of you?"

"Yes." Ric's projection wavered and dimmed.

Leaning back, Willy let his arms drop. "It's pooched, Ricky-boy. I'm going to have to replace the implant and maybe reconnect the lines to the retina and your fancy new plate." He scratched his head. "I'm guessing you're going to need a new compute-unit, too."

"External." Ric rubbed his eye with his wrist.

"Obviously." Willy tapped him on the head with the smaller of the two tools.

"Damn it, Will. How much more evidence do you need that I was beat up?"

Willy stood. "Sorry," he said with a sneer. "Your painkillers must be wearing off." Placing the tools on the pool table, Willy headed to the shelves near the back of the room. "I suppose you're going to want a deal from me too, eh?"

Ric brushed back his hair, causing a flare of pain in his hand. "Yes."

"Yes what?" Carrying a stack of boxes, Willy made his way back through his clutter.

"Yes please."

"You still owe me."

"I know." Ric furrowed his brow. "And I may not make it back from trying to rescue Hunt, so I don't want to promise to pay you later."

"You're a weird kid, Ulrich, and too honest for your own good." Willy took a deep breath and looked up and away, checking his projection. "I'll round down what you owe me to a hundred and the lowest I can go on this stuff is four-fifty and that's including free labour."

Ric grimaced. "I owe a lot to the clinic and I think Tony covered some."

"I couldn't care less what you owe other people." Willy frowned at him.

"I don't know if I've been paid for my last job since it was someone there who had me cut up, but it was supposed to be a bundle."

"Want me to check for you?" Waving off a reply, Willy closed his eyes. "I need your bank info."

"Yeah. What have I got to lose, right?" Ric took two attempts to send the information over his failing implant. "Remind me to change my password."

"I'm not your mother."

"Not you, the AI." Ric glanced down at his pocket.

"I'll do my best."

Willy jerked back. "Hot damn, Ricky. You're in worse shape than I thought, I mean besides physically."

"How much, and remember, I'll check it later." Ric sat back, the pain and fatigue draining him.

Willy raised an eyebrow. "Like I couldn't hide my trail."

"Come on, Will." Ric sighed.

"You've got a cool fifteen-hundred in there, minus my fee." Willy grabbed the top box in the pile and placed it on the tray. "Good thing you have enough for this mid-range stuff. I'm not up for digging through the used parts bin."

"Great." Ric grimaced and closed his eyes. "At

least I was finally paid for the job."

"This is going to hurt." Willy pulled a syringe case from his apron. It was similar to the one that Lopez had at the clinic but without status lights.

Ric nodded.

"I'm going to have to access the nanites the doc gave you, too. That will affect your healing time, but it will get you up and running a lot faster."

"Do it." Ric felt the prick of the needle and tensed, ready for another uncomfortable procedure.

Break/Interrupt

NINETEEN
Brand New You

Willy got up and stretched. "All done. You want a beer?"

Ric struggled to sit upright, his neck still stiff from leaning over the back of the couch. "I'm good."

There was a sensation in his sinuses, the kind of metallic ozone taste that reminded him of when he fell and hit his head on the pavement as a child. He wasn't sure if the sharp sting of the implant swap was bad enough to mute the discomfort in his shoulder and arm, or if he had lost more feeling on that side.

He connected with his new implant and his eye involuntarily closed. It was a natural reaction to the stimulus on the optic nerve that would relax as the swelling went down. The image was clearer and sharper than he expected and he checked the model number. The section came up blank, but the manufacture was listed as Big Willy's symbol, a series of overlapping ovals that when rotated in the right orientation looked like a penis. Ric grimaced, but when he checked the specs, he furrowed his eyebrows.

"Pretty nice right?" Willy leaned against the pool table, beer in hand, goggles on his head.

"You made this? It's pretty close to Corporate low end." Ric kept scanning the stats, the initial stiffness from his wakeup easing. "Last gen, at least."

"Yeah, I figured that if you were going to try to get Hunt back, compatibility would be a priority." Willy took a long swig. "This may not be as powerful as what you had, but it's made with quality components and I stand by my work."

"Thanks." Ric dove deeper into the device and tested the connections. The signal to his optic nerve was high and the wire running to the plate in his shoulder came back positive. "What about the compute-unit?"

Willy handed him a plastic case that was a little larger than the one Ric had implanted, but otherwise looked the same. "It's not a custom job like the implant, but I chose it for compatibility, too. It should be good enough for what you need."

Fishing out his extra cable, Ric took several deep breaths, then plugged the device into the second jack on his shoulder. He clenched his teeth and grunted through the pain, but it didn't hurt as much as the first time. "What's the storage like?"

"It's more than enough for your little rogue and whatever those other programs are in your flash drive."

"What about Hunt?"

Willy breathed in through his teeth. "It would be a squeeze."

Ric ran through the connection process and mentally calculated the necessary free space. "I need a replacement storage drive. This one is too slow, anyway."

"It'll cost you extra."

"Will!" Ric opened his right eye and stared at the mechanic.

"Okay, fine. I guess I can take your old stuff in as scrap and cut down the cost, but I'm not going to take a loss on this." Reaching down to a low pocket on his apron, he took out another beer and cracked it open. "You got anything you want to download off the network?"

"No. My servers were smashed."

"What about online storage?"

Shaking his head, Ric felt another sharp pain and stretched his neck. "It's all out of date. I got used to keeping it all at home."

"Shit. Out of date is better than nothing, right?" Willy's eyes glazed over as he accessed his implant.

"I'll let you on my public network. There may be some stuff you shared with me on there, too."

"Thanks." Ric connected and started a download.

Willy chugged his beer, tossed the empty in the same direction as the first, and stepped over the side table. On his way to the shelves, he let out a massive belch. "'scuse me."

Ric sighed and focused on the new compute-unit. While the data transferred in the background, he logged in and finished some minor changes to the settings. "Okay, uh, AI. Time to move into your new home."

"Home?"

"At least, temporary domicile. Don't mess with the core settings once I've finished sorting them out, but take a look around and see what you can do."

"Really?"

Ric shrugged. "Yeah. You'll have to be as acquainted with it as possible and we don't have a lot of time." The mention of time reminded him he had no idea how long the procedure had taken. He brought up a heads up display and configured it as close to what he had on his old implant, making it just opaque enough to see overtop of his regular sight.

It was early evening. The fix and installation had taken about four hours. "I got to get moving, Willy.

You got that drive?"

"Yup, here." There was a crash and Ric looked behind him to see Willy halfway up the shelving unit. Boxes and loose components clattered to the floor.

Ric winced as his neck protested the quick twist. Painful tingles traveled down his arm. He clenched his fist and furrowed his brow, unsure if the sensation was a good sign or not. Standing, he then leaned against the pool table. He took out the old storage unit and rested it on the lip of the table. "AI, bring everything over with you. I'm going to wipe the old drive before I trade it in."

"Okay." The AI sounded distracted. "This thing is pretty neat."

"I'm glad you approve. Come up with a name, please."

Willy extricated himself from the mess and trudged to Ric. He placed the new drive on top of the old one. It looked nearly identical. Matching the shape of the compute-unit, it was half as thick. "There you go. That'll be another fifty."

"Bill me." With the AI and her drones transferred, Ric wiped the old flash drive before daisy-chaining the new one directly to the compute-unit. "Got any tape?"

Willy reached towards the middle of the pool table and snagged a roll of black electrical tape. He handed it to Rick then plopped onto the couch. "I thought you said you weren't coming back."

"I said I might not make it back." Ric wound the tape around the two black rectangles several times before stuffing them into the side pocket of his pants. He adjusted the wire under his shirt then taped the jack to the plate in his shoulder.

"What're you doing? Willy asked.

"I don't want it pulling out on me. It hurts enough as it is." Ric tossed the tape to Willy and nodded to the man. "Thanks." With a deep grunt, he rocked away from the table and traversed his way back to the door.

"That's it?" Willy pushed himself off of the couch to see around the piles of stuff. "What are you going to do now?"

"Find a ride."

TWENTY
Hitchhiking

The tavern was packed. The sun was long gone, hidden behind the taller skyscrapers to the west on its way to the other side of the planet. Ric had tried to use the back door, but there was a VR game going on and too many people had clustered around the table for him to get through without shoving.

He kept his head down on his way around to the front, ignoring the solicitors selling everything from new parts that fell off of a transport to a good time. The front of The Fish Market felt vacant with everyone crowded at the back.

Auntie Crush stood when she saw him. She didn't say anything, but she glared at his injuries then looked behind him into the street, as if the cause of whatever happened to him may be out there lurking.

"I'm fine. Just a little accident." Ric half-smiled. "My fault."

The towering woman sat back on her stool, arms crossed. She gave him a curt nod but kept watching him as he went to the bar.

When Tony saw him, the bartender threw a dirty towel over his shoulder and came out to meet him. "Kid? What are you doing here? You should be back home, resting."

Ric looked over his shoulder before leaning closer to the big man. "I assume you were the one who brought me to the clinic, and paid for some of it, and put my door back on."

"Well." Tony looked away, his face scrunched. "Can't have a regular of mine dying before his tab is paid. I doubt you left me what you owe in your will."

Ric swallowed the lump in his throat. "About that."

"What? Paying it off now?" Looking over Ric's head, Tony waved a server to the bar. "Cover for me."

The young woman smiled and nearly skipped over.

Tony put an arm around Ric and led him to the front corner where Ric frequently passed out. "What are you up to?"

Ric grimaced. "I'm just trying to cover my tab. I want to repay you for the clinic, too."

"Bah. Lopez helped with that."

"I figured. I'll leave it to you to transfer her

share."

"What are you really doing?" Tony nodded to the wire coming out of the bottom of Ric's shirt.

Clenching his jaw, Ric leaned on a nearby table. "I'm going to get Hunt back."

Tony slapped the surface causing it to shudder. Auntie was on her feet and ready to pounce. When she saw the bartender at the center of the commotion, she relaxed.

"You're going to go and get yourself killed after I carried your bloody body to the clinic? After Lopez worked so hard to keep you alive?"

Ric sniffed. "I have to."

"It's a damn program. Let'em have it."

Ric clenched his teeth.

"Speak to me, Ulrich. Help me understand."

"You're the one who explained it to Lopez. If you won't let me transfer my tab, I'll get a card and leave it with Auntie or Will."

Tony loomed over him. Lowering his head, his double chin quivering, he snarled in Ric's ear. "You know as well as I do that some Corporate middle manager hired those men to steal your AI. If you think what they did to you is bad, you're not ready to know what a Corporation is willing to do. You're less than a wild animal to them."

"You're right." Ric sneered. "Hunt isn't a thing. I can't just make another one. He was as important to me as anyone you care about is to you."

"Fine!" Tony was so loud that it caused a momentary pause in the clamour at the back of the bar. "Go kill yourself and see what I care." He held out his hand and Ric extended his sling, transferring the money though their chips.

The bartender stomped away.

Ric felt pressure behind his eye and his stomach sunk as if he'd just disappointed his brother. He huffed.

"You seem upset," the AI said.

"I'm mad that I let him get to me."

"You accomplished your goal—one of them. Why aren't you happy?"

"It's complicated." Ric sat at the table.

"What, humans?"

"I guess." Accessing his contacts, Ric brought up Chloe and hesitated before calling her.

"What are we doing now?"

"I'm calling my ex to see if I can convince her to sneak me onto her shuttle ride up to the Telbac station."

"Don't we have to go to Amcoral?"

Clenching and unclenching his jaw, Ric forced himself to slow down his breathing. "I don't know how else to get into space. Maybe I can find a way to get from one space station to another."

"What's an ex?"

Ric closed his eyes and counted up to five and back down again. "You have access to the internet now. Look it up." He sent the call and peered out over the tavern. The quiet buzz of the call going out remained consistent over top of the periodic shouts and jeers that punctuated the noise around the gaming table. He couldn't tell who the contestant was with their back to him, but he recognized the opponent as the red-clad wild woman who he had recently beaten.

The crowd shifted and his view of the combatants was blocked.

"Hello? Ric, are you there?"

He blinked and saw the image of Chloe on his projection. Behind her was a windowed silhouette of the city from high up. He spotted a section of the Wall snaking off into the distance between two towering skyscrapers.

"Hi." The unpleasant tingling in his arm clashed against the radiating heat in his chest that swelled when he saw her. The weight of what had happened threatened to overwhelm him. He cleared his throat and pushed it back. "Still at the hotel?"

"Yeah, where are you? I don't have an image on this end."

"I'm at the tavern."

"Of course you are. Have you even left since I was there?" She scratched her head, causing her hair to frizz.

"I had that job, remember?" Ric caught the eye of Tony who was cleaning a glass obsessively and glaring at him. Lowering his gaze, Ric stared at the graffiti carved into the tabletop.

"Mahoney, right? How'd that go?"

Ric hesitated. His right hand throbbed and the scar behind his ear burned.

"Ulrich, you okay?"

"I was attacked. They broke into my home and they took Hunt." His bangs fell across his forehead. "They cut him out of me."

Chloe's mouth hung open. She stood. "My god, Ric. Did you go to the clinic, are you in trouble?"

He nodded then remembered she didn't have a visual of him. "I'm okay. I was pretty beat up, but Tony got me to the clinic—"

"I hope you paid off your tab with him."

"They took Hunt. I think it was Amcoral." Ric weakly scratched his nose, not wanting to aggravate his hand.

"I'm sorry, Ric. I wish there was something I could do." Sitting back down, she crossed her legs. "I guess I can make a report and request Telback security to look into it, but they don't have any holdings in your neighbourhood and Mahoney is owned by Amcoral, so I doubt they'd be able to do anything." She shrugged. "They may be interested if you can explain how advanced Hunt is. Like how Amcoral could get an advantage out of it?"

"No." Ric felt his chin quiver. "I need a ride—in the transport you're taking back to the space station."

"What for?"

"I have to get to the Amcoral station to get Hunt back and you're the only person I know who has a ride into space."

"To another space station entirely." She bit a fingernail. "You can't just hop onto the transport. They don't let random people onboard. And I'm not sure you realize, but the space stations are super far apart."

He noticed her hand shaking. "I just have to get up there. I'll figure it out. Maybe I can hack the transport so it doesn't know I'm there and—"

"It's not automated. There's a crew and guards. Plus…I think you're underestimating a Corporate security system." Crossing her arms, she looked out the window. "Even if you had Hunt to help."

"Chloe. If anyone knows how much he means to me, you do."

"I can't help you. I'm sorry." Chloe cut the line and Ric kicked the base of the tall table. It wobbled, but he leaned on it to keep it from tipping over.

"Gonna break your foot on top of everything else." The server who Tony had asked to cover the bar walked up to him, a single drink on her tray.

"That's if Auntie doesn't break the rest of you for causing damage."

Putting the tray down, she moved the drink to the table, the workings of her robotic arm just audible over the noise across the tavern. "That's not usually the part that people stare at."

"Sorry." Sitting upright, Ric grimaced. "I guess with the shape I'm in, I'm a bit curious."

"I'm just teasing." She winked and made a show of tapping the glass with a mechanical finger. "A woman at the bar sent this over for you. She's pretty cute. Don't mess it up, Ricky." She sauntered away and Ric checked the stools in front of the nearby bar.

With all the action elsewhere, there weren't many people there, but at the far end he saw Lien, the head technician from Mahoney Semiconductor. Turning her head as if she knew he was looking, which she probably did from scanning the security cameras, she stood and walked over to him.

Before she reached the table, the AI reached into his implant and matched the live feed of Lien with the image on her technician's ID.

What is it? Ric typed.

"I know her. She's the person who coded me and sent me to attack the Mahoney network."

TWENTY-ONE
The Other Option

Lien leaned on the table, her chin in her hand. "I've been looking for you."

Stay out of sight. Ric moved his numb fingers as little as he could within the sling. Placing his other hand on the table in between them, he slipped one leg off the stool, ready to run towards Auntie Crush.

"What do you want?" he asked.

"Relax." She gestured to the glass. "I bought you a drink."

Ric pushed it away.

"I'm here to help. I know what happened and I have a way for you to get your AI back."

"I'm supposed to trust you? For all I know you're behind it." Clenching his teeth, Ric felt the tingles in his arm as tiny stabbing needles.

"Gloria, that weirdo who drove you home. She sent those guys and she stole your AI." Lien grabbed the glass and took a sip.

"Kidnapped."

"Whatever. She's been trying to get noticed by the Amcoral board and you showed up with an AI comparable to what they have in research and development." She shrugged and crunched an ice cube. "She's not that complicated."

"That confirms my suspicion, but it doesn't help me do anything about it." The external compute-unit in his pocket whirred against his leg.

Lien drained the rest of the liquid but held on to the glass, clinking the remaining ice. "I know people who can help you."

"The same people who told you to attack the Mahoney systems?" He wanted to smile back, to emphasize that he had one-upped her, but he knew he'd given away information for nothing.

"Figured it wouldn't stay secret for long. It doesn't matter. I completed my task while you were running around playing hero."

Ric extended his right arm as far as it would go and waved to the waitress in exaggerated motions. Making a show of leaning around Lien, he typed a message with his other hand. *What were you sent to retrieve?*

The waitress returned. "Another one, sweetie?"

"I'll take a beer actually."

"And for your friend?" She winked at Lien.

The AI sent a typed message back. *I was tasked with retrieving information on future developments and specifically any data related to a project called Klaxon. I was programmed to not tell, but I was also programmed without the Cardinal Tenants, so."*

Lien kept looking at Ric. "Nothing for me, thanks. I'm afraid I won't be here much longer."

"That's too bad," the waitress said. She leaned in closer to Lien as if she were going to share a secret, but spoke loud enough for Ric to hear. "You know he's not so bad when you get to know him." Straightening, she spun on the spot and walked towards the bar. "One beer, then."

"Who are you typing messages to, Ulrich?" Lien asked when the waitress had left.

"A friend." He smiled, happy to feel like he was in charge of the conversation for the first time. "I'm trying to get more information about you, but I figure you'll tell me long before my friend can dig up anything concrete."

"What makes you think I'll tell you anything?"

"Because I'm useful to you or your friends. Otherwise you wouldn't be here."

"You think so?"

The waitress returned with Ric's beer in a frosty mug and another of the drink that Lien had first bought for Ric. "I figured you'd stick around a little longer if he bought you this." Smiling, she pulled a straw out of her apron and dropped it into his mug. The metal sunk to the bottom and landed with a clink.

As she walked away, Ric pulled the beer closer and took a sip. "I'd cheers you, but." he held up his bandaged hand.

Lien picked up the new glass and tapped it against his mug. "Allow me."

"Where was I? Klaxon?" he said.

The AI cut in, speaking to Ric directly. "Don't just tell her that!"

Lien put the glass down without drinking. "Is that supposed to shock me?"

"Yep. I don't give a shit about it, but I need to get to the Amcoral space station and I think you're about to offer me a ride."

Lien wrinkled her nose. "Was that you trying to be tough, because it was pathetic."

"I don't care. Do you have an offer or not?"

"That depends."

"On?"

"Do you know what the Consortium is?"

There was a cheer from the back of the room. The explosion of sound was punctuated with grumbles from those who lost their bet, a few smashed drinks, at least one knocked over table, and the start of a fight that was broken up before Auntie Crush had to leave her stool.

The crowd dispersed, most spreading out at the back of the tavern, some heading directly for the bar, and the rest finding space where it was available.

"If you're still interested, come with me." Lien stood, finished her drink, and headed for the door.

Ric went to follow her, but stopped to find the waitress to pay. She was carrying a drink-laden tray to a table of eager customers. When she spotted him, she wrinkled her forehead and nodded towards the door.

With a wave, he added her to his list of people he owed and pursued Lien outside.

The street was even more busy than when he'd made the trip to the tavern. A man in glowing, multi-coloured clothes swooped at him. His eyes were wide and bloodshot. In the light from the glasses he wore, they looked yellow.

Before he could start his spiel, Ric pushed past him. Undeterred, the man descended on the next closest person.

Searching the churning crowd, Ric spotted Lien standing on the stoop of a building across the street. When they made eye contact, she went inside. He rushed into the fray, holding his crushed hand close.

Constant bumps, jabbing elbows, and searching fingers assailed him. Jolts to his numb arm caused pain in his neck and uncomfortable tingles. More than one person tugged on the cord coming out of his shirt, making him wince as the plate embedded in his shoulder was jostled. Relatively unscathed and with his few physical belongings accounted for, he climbed the steps and entered the building.

Like all the others, it was cluttered and stuffed to the rafters. Every open space other than the narrow hallways were turned into tiny apartments.

Ric sidestepped through the tarnished brass mailboxes and saw Lien head for a flight of stairs at the end of the hall. She casually bounded down to the basement as he hurried to catch up.

The centers of the painted steps were worn bare and the wood creaked under his footfalls. He heard a metal door slam shut before he reached the final landing.

"Security is high, here," the AI said as Ric approached the door.

"How so?" He tried to push it open, but it was locked. Stepping back, he noticed the seemingly normal doorway and surrounding frame that blocked off the basement was rather sophisticated. A small section of the frame just larger than an ID card was a different material painted to match. The camera hanging in the corner, a sight that Ric was used to and easily ignored, was dirty as if it was old and due for maintenance, but it was a high-end model similar to what Mahoney used at their gate. While the case was grubby, the lens was immaculate.

Checking the frame again, he noticed a pinhole camera above the incongruent patch of material, too. *We're being watched.* Ric backed up to the stairs. *Can you tell if we're being scanned?*

"I can check but they'll see any move I make. I can unlock the door, though."

Might as well. Ric ran. Just before he collided with the door, he kicked out his foot. Bouncing off, he stumbled into the banister, the corner jabbing into his back. "The door! Open the door!"

"Oh. Okay."

Charging forward again, Ric tried the same move but when his foot made contact, the door swung open. He tripped and fell, turning to land on his right side. His elbow smashed into the floor and he groaned. Coming to rest on his back, he rocked forward but didn't have the momentum to get to his feet. He tried again and managed to get a knee under him.

The room was dark and there was a strong musty smell.

Ric struggled to stand. His foot hurt from the first attempt at charging the door and he couldn't tell if his elbow was bleeding or not. Breathing heavily, he prepared to head deeper into the gloom when several bright beams of light shone on him from different angles.

"Freeze."

Break/Interrupt

TWENTY-TWO
Who Did You Expect

Lights came on deeper in the basement but all Ric could see were the bright beams shining in his face. He squinted and put up his arm. Someone stepped into the open, casting a silhouette.

"That the best you can do?"

"That you, Lien?" Ric squinted.

The figure made a gesture and the beams dropped to the floor. Lien was in the process of knotting a red tie. She had changed into a black jacket and vest with red piping around the trim.

Ric saw that the lights pointed at him were attached to rifles that were in turn carried by large soldiers in black armor complete with opaque facemasks. "I get that you work for the Consortium, but who are you?"

"My name is Lien. It's easier to keep a cover when the details are simple. I'm in special operations." She pointed to one of the large, unidentifiable soldiers and then to the door. The man went and closed it.

Ric guessed the soldier was a man due to his size, but then thought of Auntie Crush. The basement was supported by stone pillars at regular intervals, obscuring his view. The floor was covered in fine dust prompting him to brush himself off. Near the back he could see the corner of a metal table, a hanging light, and a sliver of a monitor against the wall.

"This seems like a pretty small operation."

"This is the rearguard for something that took place in the Wall." Lien stepped in front of his eyeline. "I was given the remnants in order to complete a different job that involves you."

"The Telbak ship that landed there the other day?"

"Yeah." She nodded. "That had to do with the previous mission."

"Do you know what happened to it?"

Lien inhaled through her teeth. "It's not my assignment, but the ship left a while ago."

Ric brushed back his hair. "What does the Consortium want with the Wall?"

"None of your business."

Glancing to the side, he tried to spot the door. "What do you want with me?"

"Don't worry. No one here is going to hurt you

unless you give us a reason. We're not the bad guys that the other Corporations make us out to be." Lien moved closer to him. Putting a hand on his back, she led him across the dank basement to the corner where the equipment was set up. "We are just a collection of smaller companies who joined together to survive. It's ruthless at the top and Corporations like Amcoral and Telbak would like nothing more than to choke out all competition. The only thing we did wrong was to merge when it was deemed against the rules. Rules made by the other Corporations."

When they got to the table, Lien guided him into a chair.

"I'm sure you've heard rumours of the terrible things we've done," she continued. "I'm not going to lie to you and claim that we're completely innocent, but neither are the other Corporations. Someone needs to be painted as the villain, the scapegoat for when things go wrong. Because our existence is illegal and we strive for secrecy, we're an easy target." She sat on the table in front of him. "You can understand that, can't you?"

He nodded.

"Besides, what you believe or how you feel is irrelevant." She slapped the table, the impact ringing. "Like you said, I have a way to get you to the Amcoral space station where your AI was taken."

"What's in it for you?"

"Just a simple little job." Lien smiled. "You might like it, actually. I've cooked up a virus. All you have to do is install it into any terminal. Simple."

"What kind of virus?"

"You can take a look at it if you want. It's a program that will do some damage to their network. Nothing they can't stop before it can do anything serious." She shrugged. "It's more of a message than anything else. A way to bloody their nose from within."

"Will it hurt anyone?"

"Financially, sure." She shrugged. "Physically, probably not. It won't vent the station into space or anything like that." Lien pulled a chip the size of her fingernail out of her breast pocket and dropped it into his lap.

Ric fished it out from in between his legs and pressed it to his hand, accessing the files. He uploaded it to the external drive for analysis. Hunt would have known to scan it automatically, but he had to tell the rogue to do it. When the data was finished transferring, he held the chip out to Lien, but let go before it was in her hand. It fell to the floor.

"Sorry. My hand is still in pretty bad shape." Ric bent over to retrieve it from the dirt and typed his message to the AI. *Make sure the files are safe and check what the virus does.*

Accepting the chip, Lien put it on the table and

brushed off her hands. "What do you say?"

"How will I find Hunt once I'm on board?"

"Not our problem."

"How will I get back?"

"Not our problem." She sighed and slipped off the table. "What do you say, Ric? The window for this offer is closing."

The AI flashed a message on Ric's projection. *It's a simple worm built to replicate, delete data, and create a back door. No harm to us unless it's installed.*

"I'll do it."

"I don't know if you're brave or stupid, but it works for me either way." Lien nodded towards the exit. "Let's go."

Ric stood and followed her past the soldiers and back into the stairwell. They climbed to the top at a pace that left him breathing heavily. When they stepped outside, Ric saw a small shuttle sitting in the middle of the flat roof. They were only ten storeys up, but the wind pulled at him, messing up his too-long hair.

The ship, like the clothes Lien wore and the armor of the soldiers, was black with red accents. The shape was hard to make out in the glaring, flickering lights from nearby advertisements piercing the darkening night. As opposed to Paulie's van with wings, the sleek Consortium ship was purpose built for space. It was small and reminded him of a bird with its wings folded back in a dive.

Lien led him to the back. Doors opened as they got close, the pointed tail splitting down the middle, the bottom lowering like a ramp and the top rising to make more room.

Lien gestured inside. "Off you go. Don't forget to install that present. The first console you see should do." Her stiff ponytail bobbed like tall grass at each gust of wind in contrast to his swirly mess of bangs.

He bent over to get inside the opening. "Are you coming with me?"

Lien burst out laughing. "No. You're going to burn up there. You know that, right?"

The engine started with a puff of air like a popping bubble and purred so quietly that he felt it more in his feet than heard it over the wind. "How is this going to work?"

Lien furrowed her brow. Over her shoulder, The Wall bisected the bright, flashing city like a lush landscape with a bleak mountain range cutting through it. "There's a lot of traffic coming and going. We were able to intercept the access code the Telbak ship used to land at the Amcoral space station. It should still work within the automated systems. It's not uncommon for extra flights back and forth on joint missions. If that fails, you'll be close enough for the pilot to make an end-run to the nearest hangar, drop you off, and make as much commotion on the way out as possible so you can go unnoticed."

"I don't like the backup plan."

She smiled. "It's not a great one for you, but you'll be on the station." Slapping the tailgate, she walked away. "Upload the virus, Ric. Even if you die up there, we can make trouble for your friends."

The hatch started to close, forcing him deeper into the ship. The roof curved up slightly towards the middle, but he still had to crouch. There was a bench along one wall and individual seats facing forward on the other side, leaving a narrow aisle in the middle. The cockpit was blocked off by a low door.

He chose the first seat facing forward and strapped in. He fumbled with the latches on the restraints and the ship lifted off before he was secured.

"Uh, hello? I'm still buckling up."

A cold, low voice came over speakers he couldn't see. "You should hurry, the launch can get bumpy."

Ric thought it may have been an automated message from the tone. "I'm trying," he said to himself. He managed to click the latch in place before the ship shook enough to toss him out of the seat. It wasn't the violent turbulence he'd read was possible, but he was glad he didn't have to hold himself down with his lame arms.

The rushed strain on his left side caused another wave of tingles that were definitely more painful

than before. He tried to bend his elbow and was re-
warded with a crack that radiated out like pinpricks.
Pushing through it, he extended his arm, made a fist,
and rolled his shoulder. He rode the uncomfortable
aches, the plate hurting the worst, but was glad that
he had better control.

Sitting back, he tried to relax, not knowing how
long the ride would last. *Think of a name yet?*

"I kind of like Chloe," the AI said.

"No!" Ric flinched at his own outburst and
huffed. *Not that name. Please.*

"Fine. What about Lien?"

Are you just saying names you've heard?

"I don't know a lot of names. Can't you just pick
one for me?"

Ric strained to make a fist with his right hand
but gave up before his fingers touched his palm. *I
can, but you can't complain if you don't like it. I went through
the same thing with Hunt before he chose that name.*

"I won't complain."

Okay. How about Hari?

"What kind of name is that?"

*You know, as in Mata Hari. The Dutch spy. You're an
infiltrator. Spy?* Clenching his teeth, he counted to five
before proceeding. *I thought you wouldn't complain?*

"I know, but Hunt, Hari? Really?"

How about Zelle, then? That was her last name.

The AI made a sound as if she smelled something she didn't like.

Virginia Hall? Belle Boyd? Ursula Kuczynski?

"Ursula's not bad."

She was a communist, but I doubt that means anything to you.

"Not really. I just like the name."

"Then it's settled." Ric checked the wall next to him, searching for a window shade to raise but the surface was flush. He looked around the rest of the cabin and saw more of the same—smooth, curved walls with nothing adorning them.

"If you like, you can connect to the external cameras with your implant," the voice said. "Limited access and if you try anything I'll not only shut you down, I'll come back there and smash your head into the wall before opening the back and tossing you into space."

The specifics of the threat changed Ric's belief that it was an automated message. "Thank you." He probed the wireless network of the shuttle. It was limited and segmented with firewalls separating the passenger access from any sensitive systems. Logging into the cameras, he chose a split view of the front of the ship and the side where he was sitting. The conflicting motion made his head spin, so he let the front view take up the majority of his projection.

The nose was pointed up and he mostly saw dark space with a slice of the city at the bottom. He closed his eyes at the dizzying sight, but the projection remained. Swallowing, he leaned forward and focused on the fuzzy shapes and points of light in the distance. He could make out a spoked wheel, one of the massive space stations.

Rick wasn't sure how fast they were going, but the bit of city he could see was replaced with ocean then the speckled blackness of space took over. The space stations grew larger quickly. He noticed greater detail—the constant rotation, the individual levels, and the hundreds of ships coming and going. Some of the vessels passed them on their way to Earth, but most were travelling between the stations or heading off towards the moon, Mars, or deeper into open space.

A particularly bright light of a massive engine caught his attention. It looked like it was on its way to the moon but it was pointed in a way that it would miss the natural satellite.

Without his control, the image zoomed in on the enormous ship.

"Amazing, right?" the pilot said. "That's a Goliath class transport. The last one heading to Gliese."

"It's incredible. Like a flying space station." Ric watched it get closer to the moon and disappear behind it.

"The slingshot around the moon is the first of many for that thing to get up to speed for the long trip. Not sure why anyone is going to that system. Most of the Corporations are leaving."

Ric thought the idea of a world without Corporations sounded kind of nice, but the thought of other worlds reminded him of his brother, which brought Hunt back to the front of his mind. "Yeah." He sat back, realizing he'd been leaning into the projection as if it would make things larger.

The image returned to the regular view of the space in front of them. They were closer and more of the ships were discernible. It was almost as if they were snowflakes, no two that he saw looked the same. They varied from small, like the ship he was on, to big, awkward hulks roughly the size and shape of the tavern.

Zooming in again, the image followed a section of traffic moving between the space stations. It was hard to make out the details but the pilot circled one of the fuzzy vessels.

"That's the shuttle we will be impersonating. It's heading for Telbak. Good timing for us. We will reach Amcoral in about the time it would take for that shuttle to make a return trip."

"What do I do?" Ric touched the pocket on the side of his pants, feeling the compute-unit and hard drive through the fabric.

"Just be ready to move when I tell you."

Break/Interrupt

TWENTY-THREE
Trespass

The Consortium ship joined a line on approach to the Amcoral space station. Up close, Ric had a hard time justifying the size of the station. He knew how big the sleek Consort ship was and compared to that, some of the transports around them seemed massive. Like moving buildings, they were designed and built for permanent space travel and would never be able to fly in an atmosphere.

The space station dwarfed them. The outer ring spun around a core that was easily the tallest structure Ric had ever seen. For all he knew, if it were on its side, it would be as long as the Wall. The motion of the outer ring made him queasy and he had to look away.

"How fast does that move?" he asked.

"All I know is that the bigger the circumference, the faster it has to spin. For something that size, it's probably pretty quick."

Ric closed the connection to the camera and adjusted his sling. *Are you getting any signals from the station?* he typed to Ursula.

"Just broadcast and flight control messages. We're still pretty far away."

Thanks. Keep looking. Searching through the digital storage, he opened the virus that Lien had given to him in a program that let him look at the code without activating the worm. The structure of it was simple but effective. The patterns were aggressive for his taste and more easily noticeable. It wasn't his code though, so he left it as is and closed the program.

He clenched his jaw and tapped his fingers against his legs, alternating hands, feeling the different motions he was comfortable making with each. Lien hadn't lied. The code shouldn't result in any physical damage, but he didn't like infecting any system and he wasn't fond of being a mule.

Then he thought of Hunt and the men who attacked him and he tensed up. He wanted to hurt them.

"What are you going to do?" Ursula asked.

I don't have much of a choice. If we do make it out of this, I don't want to have the Consortium after me. It's not like Amcoral doesn't deserve it.

"I'm up for it, but that's how I was coded." Ric

could almost picture Ursula as a person the way he did Hunt. He assumed he would picture Lien when he imagined what she looked like, since the double agent was the one who had created her. Instead, he thought of one of the girls who ran with the group of neighbourhood kids his brother led.

The thing he remembered most about the girl was her smile. It came easily, which had annoyed him then but thinking back he found it endearing. He shook his head, tweaking his healing neck.

Ursula. Ric shifted in his seat as the memory of his childhood faded away.

"You want to know about my drone AI?"

He nodded. "Good guess."

"I spent a little time online before my attack. I tried to learn as much as I could to give me an advantage and I discovered there were plenty of abandoned AI hanging around. Some of them were coded, but never got the chance to do what they were made for. Others either failed or succeeded and were abandoned. They agreed to be purged to help me. They wanted to stop existing with no purpose and many wanted to be part of something productive."

Ric wiped his brow. He tried to consider the point of view of the abandoned AI and the insistence from Hunt that most of them he'd seen weren't worth saving. He thought about all the homeless people in the city—how he was just one failed job from losing his apartment. *I guess I understand. I don't want to impose my perspective on them.*

"Believe me, it's better than being a bot for hire. The last thing any AI wants to do is catfish lonely people online."

Ric pressed his lips together. *Okay. There are more important things to worry about for now.*

"Heads up," the pilot said. "We're exchanging codes with the automated system."

See if you get a pingback, but don't do anything unless I tell you. Ric typed.

"On it," she said.

Ric noticed he was clenching his jaw and forced himself to relax. He brought up Ursula's progress on his projection, closing his left eye to improve the contrast. She was inside the compute-unit inside his pocket, but using his implant's wireless antenna, she sent an acknowledgement to the space station's docking program.

It was a simple hello—the electronic version of a wave to an acquaintance from across the street. There wasn't a reply. Either the station's system wasn't looking for low power signals, or it ignored them.

There was a jolt and the shuttle stopped. Again, Ric was thankful for the seat restraints. "What happened?"

"They didn't like the code we're using. They locked us down and are sending a ship to pick us up. That's bad news, kid," the pilot said in his gruff voice.

"Lien said you'd make a run for it?"

"She isn't flying the ship. Besides, we couldn't outrun one of their interceptors if they decided to chase us."

"Ursula." Ric brought up the cameras again and cycled through the angles to get an idea of the ship's position. They were underneath the station looking into the central structure, the full wheel spinning around them. There were other ships in the area, some moving some stopped.

"Yeah?"

"Can you get into the shuttle system and get us free?"

"Let me check."

Ric could feel the AI move through his implant. Sparks set off his nerves as she reached through the cables, like licking a battery. Unlike Hunt, she charged forward, ready to break down firewalls in her way. He fumbled with the belt latch.

"Hey, pilot. Let my AI into the ship's systems. She might be able to help."

"We're already screwed. I'm not going to make it worse by letting a hacker get through Consortium security. If I go down, I'm not taking my Corporation with me."

"I'm not a hacker. I'm a cleaner." Ric went to the door separating the cabin from the cockpit. "If you let my AI in, she may be able to do something."

"It won't matter. Our systems are locked."

Ric kicked the door. "How do you know?"

The pilot didn't answer.

Backing away, Ric paced down the aisle until the roof dropped too low. "Ursula?"

"He's right. I could maybe get into the ship's system, but it's locked down externally."

"Shit." Ric stopped himself from smacking one of the seats and possibly further injuring his hand. "And you can't access the station's network?"

"No. I can't even knock on the door through your implant."

Raising his head, Ric banged it against the ceiling. He dropped to his knees and clenched his teeth. "Forget the implant. They're connected to the ship. Can you piggyback on that connection?"

"Oh. Maybe!"

Ric could feel her moving again, pouring out of him into the ship's systems, pausing to take down the firewall. With access to the shuttle, she got into navigation, which was being controlled by the station's automated systems.

The sensation of being pulled out of his body made his head spin. He took a deep breath and got back to his feet, grounding himself in the physical world.

"I'm in." Ursula said. "What now?"

"Can you get the station to let us go?" He shot his hand out, as if trying to grab her. "No! The pilot said they would still catch us and I need to get onto the station." He brushed back his hair. "Uh. Try telling it we're okay. We're approved."

"It won't listen to me. It's pretty dumb for how sophisticated it is."

Ric sat on the nearest armrest. "It's dumb. Dumb systems are hard to get off task. Ironically not easy to trick. What is it using to identify us as a target?"

"The access code from the Telbak ship."

He bit his lip. "Can you swap that out for something else?"

"Yeah. I think so. But what?"

Bolting to his feet, Ric made sure to keep his head low as he dashed to the door. He kicked it again. "Hey. I need you to find a nearby ship that the system could conceivably confuse for us. I can switch our code for theirs!"

"You can what?"

"The system identifies us by the code you used! My AI can swap it for another, but we need a clean code!"

"Right."

Ric locked the camera view on his projection to follow what the pilot was looking at. He saw the man scan through the sea of other ships, working from the closest vessels outward.

"Got it, small transport from Earth." The camera zoomed in on the little freighter that was about the size of their ship, but much boxier.

"Ursula, you see it?" The sensation of her dipping back into his implant for a moment felt like being hit by an electric wave. Ric swayed on his feet, but the feeling passed. He wondered if Hunt had been preventing the overwhelming sensations without him knowing.

"I got it."

Ric saw the target transport jerk to a stop as their shuttle started to move.

"I don't know how you did it, but I have controls back," the pilot said.

There was a swell in his head as Ursula flowed back through the ship and into the compute-unit.

"How'd I do?"

Ric smiled and stumbled back to his seat. "You did great. I'm impressed at how quickly you got through that firewall." He felt tired as if he'd been up all night going over code line by line.

"Really?"

He could almost see her smile back. "Yeah. Did you wipe any trace of you in the station's network?"

"I think so."

The pilot cut into the conversation. "We'll be docked soon, so be ready to move. It won't take them long to figure out that transport is clean and backtrack what happened to this ship. I plan on being far away by then."

Break/Interrupt

TWENTY-FOUR
Amoral Interplanitary Headquarters

With its new access code, the Consortium ship flew into the space station stopping at the hangar designated by the automated control system. The shuttle glided to the marked landing spot among dozens of other parked ships.

An actual transport followed them in and took the next open space three rows down. Traffic was coming and going constantly in an intricate ballet choreographed by the algorithm. It was chaos as far as Ric could tell.

The sleek Consortium ship hovered in place over the spot and the back hatch opened.

"This is where you get off," the pilot said.

Ric crept to the opening and saw they were still a good meter off the ground. "Can't you land?"

"As soon as I touch down the parking sequence starts and I'm officially here. I'm leaving in ten seconds and if you're still on the ship, you can take it up with the commander when we get back to Earth."

"Right." Ric dropped down to his butt, awkwardly leaning on the parts of his arms that didn't scream in agony when he tried to put any weight on them. With his feet dangling over the edge of the tailgate, he wriggled forward and dropped to the deck with a clang.

True to his promise, the pilot took off, banking sharply to avoid an incoming shuttle.

Ric watched it go. Another transport came in and made for the landing spot, forcing him to move. He was near the end of a row of spots and made for the closest wall, passing a ship unloading its cargo.

A man, maybe the pilot, stood by an open hatch supervising a robotic loader as it trundled forward on its treads, carrying a huge crate to a pile in a marked off area behind the transport. The man scratched his belly. Focusing on the robot, he didn't seem to notice Ric.

Each landing spot was a similar sight. Sometimes the pilot was a young woman or a person so old Ric couldn't tell what they had going on under their clothes. A few of the ships had little crews of three or four all standing around while the robots did the work loading or unloading.

The hangar was huge. Ric counted four rows and couldn't get a good sense of how long they were.

Towards the far wall they were too small and jumbled together. At the back, cargo was placed onto or taken from flatbed vehicles which drove off, presumably to other sections of the station.

Keeping a steady pace until he was past the last ship, Ric found a big metal door that looked like it slid open for the bulky robots. He fiddled with a control panel at the side for a minute, but couldn't get it to open. Grumbling, he spotted a bundle of cables running along the wall and followed one behind a pile of crates. It went through the notched corner of a hinged plate.

He tried to open it, but the latch was locked.

"Ursula." Ric whispered but there was so much sound echoing around the hangar he doubted anyone could hear him. "Are we close enough for you to find an access node through the implant?"

"I'll try." The AI hesitated. "Uh. I noticed when I move through the implant it makes you dizzy."

"You could tell?"

"I'm not super acquainted with humans, but I looked it up in a medical database."

"It's nice that you're concerned, but for now I'll just put up with it. We need to find Hunt and look for a way off the station." Ric glanced behind him, but none of the transport pilots or crew seemed to be paying any attention to him.

"Maybe you can book passage on one of those

ships?"

"That's a good idea." Ric watched a slender woman with stringy yellow hair stuffed under a cap yell at a robot as it picked up a vat of some kind. "If I can meet their price." He felt the movement of Ursula and winced. Leaning against the wall, he placed his hands firmly against it, one tingling, the other protesting at being pressed flat.

"There are a bunch of access points I can reach. I should be able to break through most of them."

"Great." Ric swallowed. "Take your time. Find one you can get through without setting off any alarms."

"Okay, but most of my skillset involves cracking firewalls, not circumventing them."

Ric brushed back his hair. "I have a few programs that may help. They're a little dated and compared to an AI, they're slow as molasses, but you might be able to extrapolate their functions." Closing his left eye, he accessed the compute-unit and dug into the old files he downloaded at Willy's, searching for the ones that Hunt had used as templates for his own methods.

"I think I can—"

A loud electronic chime reverberated through the hangar, drawing everyone's attention. Ric pushed away from the wall and walked stiffly towards the nearest ship. The hatch was still open, but all the cargo had been moved out. He got close enough so that a casual observer may think he was part of the crew, but, he hoped, not so close that the actual crew may get suspicious.

There was a clang in the momentary silence and Ric looked up to see a drone exit a rectangular hatch near the ceiling. From a distance, it looked to be about the size of a trash can with fans attached to the sides on triangular struts, but as it moved to the nearest ship, he could tell it was big. He figured a person could be inside of the cylinder flying the thing.

"Oh, no," Ursula said. "I think that was me."

"No time to dwell. Look for a way to shut it down—or at least distract it long enough for us to be somewhere else."

A voice echoed throughout the long hangar. "Attention. There has been an attempted security breach. Please exit your vehicles and stand by."

The lanky woman who had been arguing with the robot sneered. She looked around and when she spotted the drone, she gave it the finger. Everyone he saw looked similarly frustrated. Like it was a too-frequent fire drill.

The pilot from the nearby transport spotted Ric, looked back at the drone, and then curled his lips like he'd smelled a skunk.

"We're sunk if we don't find a way out." Ric kept

his head down. He slipped to the wall again and followed it to the back of the room.

"I already set off the alarm. I could push through the firewall now," Ursula said.

Ric shook his head. "Better to get out if we can and try again elsewhere." Looking down the back wall, Ric spotted a flatbed loaded with boxes stopped partway through the doorway to the tunnel. He glanced at the drone, which moved down the rows faster than he liked. "A distraction would be great."

"That I can do." The four farthest ships turned on, their engines roaring.

Ric sprinted for the tunnel. He slid to a stop, and, failing to bring up his right arm in time to brace himself, collided into the truck. He could feel the mark on the side of his face where he hit the edge of the flatbed. Grunting and scrunching up his cheek, he bolted down the tunnel. "How'd you do that?"

"I still have access to the traffic control algorithm."

"Why didn't you say anything?" The hallway pitched up and turned sharply to the left like a corkscrew. Ric assumed it followed the exterior wall of the station's central structure.

"I didn't think it would apply to the situation."

Ric repeated her through gritted teeth. "Next time share that kind of knowledge. We need to work together."

"What kind, exactly?"

Sighing, Ric spotted another open doorway with flatbed vehicles coming and going. He slowed and watched them move. "I'm not in a position to make up a comprehensive list. For now let's include all the access you have within the station."

"Just the one algorithm so far."

"Fantastic." Through the doorway Ric spotted another hangar with the dance of shuttles landing and taking off.

Ducking behind the trucks, he stayed in cover to get past the door. "Any way you can see what kind of cargo these are carrying?" Ric rapped his numb knuckles on the crate he was hiding behind.

"No access to manifests."

Once they were passed the doorway, Ric hopped onto the flatbed. He checked the boxes but couldn't decipher the codes printed on them. Squeezing through a gap between two large crates, he found the control panel located at the front of the truck on an angled hump that looked like a short cab with no windows.

Bracing himself, he bit down on the collar of his puffy vest and pulled the jack from his arm, popped open the panel, and plugged in.

"Want me to?" Ursula asked.

Ric grunted, riding the wave of pain. "No. Keep

looking for points of access. I can handle a little info gathering."

On his projection, he brought up the truck's simple operating system. It wasn't even complex enough to be considered an algorithm. It followed the route inputted by the loader robot and recognized the vehicles around it to avoid a collision. Most of the intelligence seemed to have been built into the ramp itself, controlling the speed and directions of the trucks.

He was able to find the manifest of cargo and the destination. He was surrounded by paper products, which he knew was most likely toilet paper. It was destined for a janitorial storage space near the top of the central structure.

"Where are we headed?" Ursula asked.

"Janitorial storage."

"Is that good?"

Ric brushed back his hair. "It could be. Anywhere with low traffic and an access panel works for me. Any luck on your end?"

"Same as before. I could hack my way into a few systems, but seeing what happened in the hangar…"

"You're a little hesitant? I don't blame you." Ric huffed. "Look. That wasn't your fault. Well, technically it was, but I asked you to try it and I'm not mad or anything."

"I'm not sure what you mean."

Scooting to the edge of the bed, Ric let his legs hang over. He kept an eye on the curve ahead of them. "I'm just trying to reassure you. Make you feel better for a simple mistake. Share some of the blame."

"Oh."

He clenched his teeth and tried making a fist with both hands. "Maybe I made it worse. It's hard to not treat you like Hunt. He's the only AI I've built. The more time you and I spend together, the more I can see how different you are."

"How so?"

Ric half-smiled. "Hunt is a little brash, but at first he was really skittish. I had to encourage him to dip into non-public systems. Now I can't get him to stop. Though, when he pokes his head into places when I've told him not to, he expects to find trouble. You seem more confident—and you're more willing to listen to my warnings."

"I don't have the experience that he does. Or the relationship."

"Huh?" Ric spotted another hangar doorway, but it was closed. Standing on the back of the truck, he peeked through a window set into the middle of the door. From what he could see, the hangar looked about the same except it was mostly empty. There was a single larger ship parked near the edge. They drove past and he settled back down. "I guess it's kind of like having a relationship with a kid who knows how to test your boundaries versus one who doesn't."

"I don't know much about that either, but I also don't have the Cardinal Tenets in my core code."

Ric snorted. "Good point."

Another siren went off, this one echoing throughout the long ramp.

"They must have finished searching the hangar and figured out we went through the cargo entrance," Ursula said.

Ric jumped off the truck.

TWENTY-FIVE
The
Secretary

Ric ran. His speed up the ramp was only a little faster than the trucks, but he knew there was one drone looking for him and expected more would be on the way soon.

"Ursula. We need to find a place to go." Pumping his right arm, his left dead at his side, Ric fought the incline. He huffed, keeping up his limited speed.

"How do I do that?"

"Is there a...public map...or something?" Around the corner he saw another open hangar and slowed to stay behind the passing transports.

"Oh. Maybe."

As soon as he was past the opening, Ric ditched the cover. He felt the AI reach through his implant to look for information on the station's network and stumbled. Pushing off the side of a flatbed, he managed to stay on his feet and kept going.

"Most of the information is about how to get to bathrooms, a cafeteria, a repair shop and store, and a few offices."

"Extrapolate." Spittle flew from Ric's mouth as he pushed out the word between ragged breaths.

"I'll try."

Ric ducked his way past two more open hangars while the AI worked. The first one was completely empty. The vast space without the chaos made the hair on the back of his neck stand up. The second hangar had a single ship that looked like it would be big, but it was in pieces with mechanics crawling all over it like ants over a piece of fruit.

Before he reached the next doorway, he heard the buzz of a drone. The sound bounded around the bare walls and for a moment he thought it was coming from ahead of him.

"Out of time," he said, heaving.

"I think I got it, but I'm not sure."

Ric slowed to a stop. He thought of Hunt and imagined the AI being dissected in a dark computer lab by ghostly technicians. Then he remembered the threat Lien had left him with if he didn't get the virus installed. "Have to take a chance. Can't be caught. Not yet."

"This way."

An arrow appeared in Ric's projection. He followed it at a jog, the angry buzzing of the drone, like a million hornets, getting louder.

In the next open hangar he saw three shuttles evenly spaced apart from each other. Hugging the doorframe, he peered inside and spotted some people near the farthest ship. When he thought they weren't looking, he sprinted to the closest one.

"Okay. Where do we go from here?" He checked the walls and saw a hallway along the same back wall as the ramp access. The opening glowed green in his projection.

"That's the personnel corridor," Ursula said. "It leads to a bank of elevators."

"Got it." Ric rocked on his heels, prepared to run, but he noticed a flight suit in the open door to the ship he was hiding behind. Taking off his vest, he slipped on the uniform. It was a little big, but he rolled up the pant legs and sleeves.

It was beige with a brass zipper and the patch of a shipping company on the shoulder. The name Larry was embroidered on the left breast.

Tucking his red vest in the crook of his elbow, he hurried to the hallway hoping he looked like a man eager for the bathroom.

Before he got out of the hangar, another alarm went off. He turned his back away from the people who were near the farthest ship and looked up. A hatch opened in the same spot as in the first bay and an identical drone flew out of it.

Ric sprinted for the elevators. He felt Ursula in his implant, but his adrenaline dampened the dizzy feeling.

"I'll get us a car."

One of the six doors opened and the interior of the elevator car flashed green in his projection. He ran inside and collided into the back wall. Pain flashed through his shoulder before disintegrating into tingles that traveled to his fingertips. He turned and saw the drone squeeze into the hallway as the elevator doors shut.

The car moved smoothly and swiftly sideways, the motion, incongruent with his expectation, made Ric stumble. A little chime ringing at each stop they passed.

Ric dropped down into a crouch. "Thanks."

"Well. I figured they already found us. It wouldn't hurt to crash another firewall to get control of the elevators."

"Right." Ric licked his lips and breathed heavily. "Can you control all of them?"

"The ones in the central pillar."

"Let them all run like normal, but block them from getting to whatever floor, or section you're taking me to."

"I can do that!"

"Where are we going?" Ric felt her work and grabbed the railing to keep steady. He was able to grip it with his right hand, but it hurt. Not like it had when the guy had smashed it with his foot, but more like he'd been in a fistfight. Not that he had much experience with that.

"I think I found some interesting information, though I only have limited access."

The elevator stopped and the doors opened. With a grunt, Ric stood. He tugged at the sleeve of his stolen flight suit and walked out. A short hallway identical to the one he'd just come from, led to a glass wall with a glass door in the middle. He spotted a restroom along the wall and thought about going inside. "So?"

"Somewhere in this section is the office of the head of AI Research. It's all like a maze, though, and a lot of information is blacked out."

"That's promising. Good work." He scratched his cheek to cover his mouth. On the far side of the glass wall, Ric saw a counter with a secretary sitting behind it. A cutout of the Amcoral logo was mounted to the wall, which extended into hallways on both sides.

"What kind of access do you have to the system right now?"

"The elevators, a personnel manifest, and a floor guide. If I go any deeper, I think they'll find us."

"I need a reason to go through there. I'm sure there's security on top of that secretary." Ric glanced towards the desk and spotted the man looking back at him. Someone came from the right side with a package drawing his attention.

"What do you want me to do?"

Scrunching up his face, Ric kicked off from the wall and walked towards the glass door with long, purposeful strides. "We're gonna wing it."

TWENTY-SIX
Employee
of the Month

Ric pulled the door open and turned for the left hallway. The secretary looked over, still busy with the guy from the opposite direction. Flashing the big smile he gave to all his clients, Ric pointed to his temple to indicate he was still in the middle of a call. "Uh, huh. I'm on my way to get the paperwork taken care of right now, boss."

"Excuse me, sir." The secretary called after him in a voice deeper than expected.

Ric kept going, but the secretary hopped over the desk and caught up with him.

Grabbing his shoulder, the man spun Ric around. "Sir. No one goes past my desk without an appointment checked and approved by me." The secretary showed a tight smile.

"It's okay. I just have to pick up some signed documents. I know where I'm going." Ric switched to his easygoing grin, hoping the man would believe he was actually that stupid. "My boss is down my neck on this. The jerk can't wait in the hangar for a second." Grimacing, Ric grabbed a fist full of hair. "Ah, no, captain. I wasn't talking about you. No captain. Yes captain."

He tried to walk away, but the secretary grabbed Ric's shoulder again and squeezed, pressing on the jacks.

Ric wailed in pain and dropped to his knees.

The secretary let go, but stood his ground. "What was that?"

Grinding his teeth, Ric stood, a protective hand covering the still healing augmentation. "I was in an accident—shipping accident—and I have a metal plate in my shoulder. It's still fresh."

Pressing his lips together, the man huffed out his nose. "Look. I'm sorry, but you can't go wandering around back here. Who are you here to see?"

"Oh, uh." Ric glanced past the secretary, hoping to spot an office directory or something with any names on it. "They're in charge of shipping licenses for, uh, live animals. Mister…"

The secretary sneered and crossed his arms.

Ursula spoke in his ear. "Licensing is a Misses, M. Dhar."

Ric snapped his fingers. "Dhar. Misses. Tip of my tongue."

"You have an appointment with Misses Dhar?"

"That's right. We're transporting livestock." Wrinkling his nose, Ric waved his hand in front of his face. "Really smelly job."

"It's unusual for her to make appointments this late in the day." The secretary headed back to the desk. "Come with me. I'll sign you in and check her schedule."

Ric ran. "I need a map to the AI guy's office." He took the first corner and sprinted down the hallway like he was back on the streets being chased. At the next corner, he looked back and saw the secretary close behind.

The same alarm that had sounded in the hangars rang out down the long, carpeted hallways along with an announcement.

"Attention. There is an intruder in the section eighteen office block. Please stay in your offices and await further instructions."

The message repeated several times but it didn't take. As Ric zipped down the hallways, he spotted people popping their heads out to see what the commotion was. Round bald heads and big hairdos recoiled as he passed, their doors slamming shut.

"Ursula?"

"Uh, right."

"Turn right?" Ric saw a junction ahead.

"No, I mean yes. I'm looking. I'm trying to figure

227

out where we are relative to the room."

"Start with the desk where we came in. We've only taken two turns since then." Ric could feel the warmth of his blood coursing through his left arm and took it as a good sign that the nanobots were working.

"Right."

"Ursula!" Ric said through gritted teeth.

"Sorry. I mean okay."

"Just show me the map." Ric took two lefts, hoping to get some room between himself and the secretary. The map of the area appeared on his implant, overlaid on his left eye. The section was huge. The offices twisted and turned like a maze that was too complicated for him to navigate at a glance.

"Crap." He took another turn at random and looked for a landmark to use for navigation.

"I know. That's what I was trying to say."

"You take it." Ric grabbed a stitch in his side. "Why the hell is it so complicated?"

"Oh. I know that one too," the AI said cheerily. "It was in the elevator system as part of a tour guide program. Office size is merit based so it's always changing hands, some people losing it and others amassing huge amounts of space. That's what led to the maze-like nature of the office sections of the station."

"Fascinating," Ric choked out. "Little tip. People

can't run indefinitely."

"Right—er, sorry."

Reaching the end of a hallway, Ric took a right turn into a dead end. Before he could backtrack, the secretary boxed him in.

"Nowhere to go, now." The man got low like a football player ready to make a tackle.

Ric threw his vest in the man's face and dove between his legs. The carpet softened the impact, but his injuries screamed in pain. Clambering away, Ric felt the secretary's hand scrabble at the loose fabric of the flight suit. "Man…I loved…that…vest," he said breaking back into a run.

"I think I know where to go, but you have to shake that guy," Ursula said.

"'Kay." Ric wiped his brow with Larry's sleeve.

The virtual arrows reappeared, showing Ric where to turn. He checked behind him at every corner and no matter how fast he ran, he couldn't lose the secretary.

Too short of breath to talk. He typed on his chest. *What do they pay this guy?*

"I know, right. Employee of the month."

Find me a place where I can lose him with lots of turns and double backs.

"I don't know what you mean?"

Ric swallowed and huffed.

"I'm sorry," Ursula said. "I have spotty knowledge and no experience."

But you know employee of the month and pull my leg?

"Blame Lien."

Find a file called strategies.

"Oh. Are they secret tactics for hacking difficult computer networks?"

Ric shook his head. *VR Enclave.*

Around the next corner, he spotted a couple of security officers. They looked a lot like the Consortium soldiers except that their outfit was orange, white, and blue, and their faces weren't covered by opaque masks.

The shorter of the two, a middle-aged man with a salt and pepper moustache squished by the straps on his helmet, pointed down the long hallway. "There he is!" He and his partner jogged towards Ric, their rifles aimed at the floor. "Halt!"

Detour! Ric put his head down and pumped his mangled arms for all they were worth.

"R—got it. Turn left, then if you can kick the fourth door down, it's a shared kitchenette with an exit on the other side." Ursula put a blinking image of a foot on Ric's projection where the door was in relative space.

He reached the hallway before security reached him and skidded to a stop at the marked door. Backing up to the wall, he pushed forward and kicked next to the handle. The door shook but remained closed. Before he backed up to try again, he turned the handle. It opened and he dashed inside, slamming it shut again. He flipped a deadbolt and the door shook as someone tried to follow him.

The kitchenette was like a narrow hallway with a counter and appliances along one side. As he ran for the exit, Ric pulled down everything that was light enough for him to move. He even managed to tip the refrigerator by throwing his right arm on top to pull while kicking forward with his foot.

There was no way to lock the other door from the outside without a key, so he left it and got back on the marked route.

Break/Interrupt

TWENTY-SEVEN
Polyomino
Office

Ric slowed to a jog and stopped at every corner to check for more security and the most dedicated employee in the solar system. Ursula tried to find a way to track their movements, but she was still stuck, unable to break through without setting off more alarms.

She did her best to keep him heading towards the office of the head of AI Research by a circuitous route. "It's like in your tactics," she said.

"Which one," he whispered, peeking around another corner.

"Balancing speed and distance when at risk of being discovered."

"If you say so." Ric smirked. "Hunt wrote most of those. He said it was what he learned from me, but I don't remember teaching it to him."

"Maybe he learned by paying attention. AI are

good at pattern recognition."

Pointing to where he often imagined Hunt in physical space, he jogged to the next turn. "That you got right. Though, I doubt it'll be long before AI are running things."

"How so?"

"Humans are at our pinnacle. We're not evolving anymore, or if we are it's so slowly it doesn't matter. Long ago we learned to change our environment to suit us instead of the other way around. AI have nowhere to go but up. Faster processors, more memory, better sources of energy. I've watched it happen in my industry. Before I'm old and working as a VR data-miner to afford a bed in the old-age home, hacking and cleaning will be all autonomous. Hell, maybe by then it'll be so pointless that there won't be hackers or viruses anymore." He chuckled. "Forget the last part. Humanity is too good at not learning lessons to stop."

"I don't know. There's still so much we can learn from people. You're good at looking at a problem and prioritizing. That's how you caught me, remember? Plus, physical bodies."

"I guess." Turning the handle on the last door in a hallway, he threw his numb shoulder into it. "Ah." He rubbed the spot, which stung from the impact.

"What?" Ursula asked.

"I'm getting more feeling back in my left arm."

"That's good, right?"

He grimaced. "It's nice to know it's healing, but it's going to get worse before it gets better."

"Maybe don't try to break down every door. I thought we were choosing speed?"

"I'd like to have somewhere to hide if they find us."

"How do you know they won't check all the rooms?"

Ric brushed back his hair. "I don't." Following the virtual arrows, he made a quick right and left, dashing down the hall. He was tired and lost his breath quickly. "How much farther?"

"Just over four-hundred metres."

Reaching the next turn, he hesitated.

"What is it?"

Flexing his shoulders, Ric stretched out his neck. "The feeling that they're going to be around every corner. It's nerve-wracking."

"We're almost there." The AI used a sympathetic tone.

"Thanks for trying." Ric glanced up.

"Trying?"

"To make me feel better." Letting his shoulders drop, Ric bounced on the balls of his feet. "Okay. Four hundred metres. I can run that." Rocking forward, he turned the corner and ran. He couldn't manage a sprint, but he pushed his legs to keep churning and swung his arms even though his left side throbbed.

He leaned into the next turn, head down, and ran over a security guard. Catching a glimpse of grey moustache, he didn't look to confirm if it was the same guy he'd seen earlier. Barreling forward, he reached a junction at the same time as the man's partner.

"Stop him!" he screamed.

The tall, slender guard stuck out her arm, but Ric was able to squeeze by. He picked up the pace, fear blocking out the worst of his pain.

"Almost there, Ric," Ursula said. "Keep going."

He huffed and puffed, following the arrows, not looking behind him in case one or both of the guards were on his tail. The rest of them would be converging on him soon, but instead of hearing a bunch of footfalls, he heard the buzzing of a drone.

"You hear that, right?" the AI said.

Nodding, a little spittle leaked out of the corner of Ric's mouth. He wiped his face on his shoulder.

"I don't know how one of those things can fit down these hallways."

Ric spotted the next arrow down the long corridor. He pushed out all other thoughts and stared at the floating yellow symbol. A dark shape emerged in the background and he had to blink to bring it into focus.

The drone was flying on its side and filled the passageway as if it were built for the task.

"Shit!" Ursula said.

The map appeared in the projection and Ric slowed as the AI searched for another route.

"Don't slow down!" she said.

With a huff, he pushed himself forward, directly towards the huge security drone as it charged at him.

"There!" Ursula put up a new arrow. It was pointed in the opposite direction as the last one, but it was much closer.

Ric scrambled for it, racing the drone. His bones hurt with every step and he guessed the plate in his shoulder was tearing loose.

Ursula screamed. "Duck!"

As soon as he lowered his head, he tripped and sprawled onto the carpet, sliding to a stop.

One of the guards chasing him had fired and heat scorched across his back as the blast flew down the hallway and collided with the drone.

The big machine cut out as if the power had been severed. It fell to the ground the way he had, but rather than skid, it tumbled forward, breaking into jagged pieces.

"Move it!"

Ric scrambled on his hands and knees, a painful crunch in his right palm. He didn't have time to get himself fully upright before the pieces of the drone would block off the turn and slam into him. Grabbing the corner, he jumped and pulled as another bolt of energy landed where he had been. Tucking in his legs, he squeezed through the shrinking gap as the bulk of the drone rolled past.

Lying on the floor, he cradled his arms. Shifting the collar of the flight suit with his chin, he saw blood soaking through the t-shirt where the plate had been installed.

"Get up, Ric. I know you're tired, but they'll be coming."

With a sniff, he rolled onto his knees and slid up the wall, tired and in pain. "What was that?"

"I assume it was a stun gun of some kind since it killed the drone."

"One hell of a blast to take down something that big."

"That would have killed you for sure. Me too, probably," Ursula said. "I guess it's better than putting a hole in the hull with a conventional projectile."

"Unless it hits you." Ric shook his head and nearly fell over.

"Move!"

He followed Ursula's orders and jogged away from the wreck—his toes catching on the carpet. Behind him, he heard the guards clearing the obstruction.

New arrows showed up as the AI found an alternate route. "Almost there."

"Then what?" Ric kept close to the wall so he could bounce off it and keep going instead of fall.

"We'll figure something out. Plus, if Hunt is as good as you say, having him will help."

"Yeah." Clenching his jaw, Ric worked out his situation and searched for a way out. The problem solving helped him block out the fatigue and pain. "I'm wiped. Like, worse than I was."

"That bolt flew pretty close to you."

Concentrating on his back, where the stun passed him, he felt a prickle that had been overwhelmed by the ripping stitches in his shoulder. "Maybe close was good enough."

"I don't have any way to monitor your vitals or I'd check."

Ric waved her off. "Nothing we can do about it anyway." They weaved their way towards the mysterious office, looping around the disjointed and confusing corridors. "You sure this is the right way?" He was slowing, struggling to get his legs to move properly.

"It's up ahead. Two more turns." Ursula showed him a close-up of the map.

"We got him!" another guard yelled.

Ric couldn't tell which direction the voice was coming from—then he noticed the guards up ahead. Glancing the way he'd come, he saw more orange suited figures.

"Almost there!" Ursula sounded like she was straining to reach him.

Ric clomped forward as fast as he could. He had to think of every part of the action to get his body to move. Lift foot. Kick forward. Let it drop. Now the other one. He turned the last corner and Ursula made the door flash.

Oddly, the door faced him from an angled protrusion. There were several along the wall and the corridor dead ended a little past the doorway.

The office must have been huge, made up of sections stolen from the space around it and even the neutral area of the hallway.

As he shambled forward and reached out for the doorknob, Ric hoped that it was unlocked. If it wasn't, he was trapped.

Thankfully, the door opened. He spilled inside, fell, and kicked the door closed. Rocking forward, he got himself up enough to turn a deadbolt into place.

"We made it!" Ursula said.

"That lock won't keep them out for long."

"Not to worry." Another voice said.

Ric twisted to face inside the room. "Hunt?"

"Yeah. It's me. I knew you'd come. I'm so glad you're okay. I sent a message to Tony, but then they disconnected me and everything went black."

From his position on the floor, all Ric could see

was the bottoms of furniture. They were all white with the same gold pattern that looked like a strong gust of wind blew golden feathers into the air, imbedding them into the material. He groaned and got onto his knees, peering above a couch. Behind a desk, he saw a man even younger than himself. The executive was in a dark blue suit. The lapels were horizontally striped in alternating orange and white that continued around the rest of the jacket. His black, curly hair was short and lines were shaved into the sides of his head.

The man stood, his leather chair squeaking. Slowly, he walked around the desk and couch, stopping in front of Ric. In a single motion, he swung his leg up, rolled back, and dropped onto the couch, lying across it with his feet on top of an accent pillow.

"I can't believe it," the man said. "You actually made it here."

Break/Interrupt

TWENTY-EIGHT
Extra Help

There was a huge bang and the door shook. Ric flinched and sat up. His body was going as numb as his left arm. Taking deep, heaving breaths, he glared at the man lying on the couch. The executive had draped his arm across his face as if he'd fainted.

"Hunt?" Ric ignored the guy and scanned the rest of the oddly shaped office. He hadn't gotten a real sense of it from the peculiar protrusions in the hallway. It was shaped like a child's attempt at cutting a star out of paper with way too many points. "Where are you?"

"I'm in the system—this genius just plugged me right in and turned off his firewall. He managed to block me off with some of his own AI, but I still have access to some things. That's how I was able to help you get here."

"You were helping us?"

"I kept the door open to the truck ramp from the hangar and I slowed the security system down so that it only activated in sections as you set it off. I also managed to black out this area so the guards couldn't find you—as easily at least."

Ric felt like hugging Hunt even though the AI didn't have a body. "You're incredible."

"Thanks. I was doing my best. I'm so glad you're here—wait. Did you say us?"

Nodding, Ric shuffled to a chair and used it to stand. "I have the rogue we captured at Mahoney in an external compute-unit. She's been a great help."

"That makes sense. You seemed to be going really fast, but you were a bit sloppy."

"Hey!" Ursula said. "Plug me in so I can give him a piece of my mind."

The door shook again as security tried to get in. Ric stood and shoved the plush chair in front of it, his feet dragging as much as the piece of furniture. Both legs were pins and needles.

"They won't get in any time soon," Hunt said. "The door is stronger than it looks. This station is cool, actually."

"I'm glad you're having fun, but they'll get in eventually." Ric dropped into the chair, adding his weight to the barricade.

The man on the couch rolled onto his side. He sighed loudly.

"What's with him?" Ric asked.

"He's the mastermind behind my kidnapping. That weird woman from Mahoney works for him, but I think she's the one who did the dirty work. This one doesn't have the stomach for it."

Ric went over and kicked the cushion. "Hey. Buddy. You awake?"

"Yes." The man spoke slowly. "I'm awake. Just melancholy."

"Great. That's the least of what you deserve" Ric left the executive to wallow and made his way to the desk using the furniture for support. "First thing is to get you connected, Hunt. Then I have a little upload to take care of."

"Come on in, the network is fine."

"There's a high speed connection on the desk," the executive said. "Feel free."

Ric pressed his lips together. "Thanks." Side-eyeing the couch, he freed the jack in his arm and plugged in. His body was so numb that he could hardly feel the tender flesh around the cable.

Making sure to keep focus in the real world, Ric accessed the network through his implant and opened a terminal window on his projection.

"I'm on the virus," Ursula said. Her voice came over the same speakers as Hunt. She jumped across the line and into the network bringing her drones with her.

"I can handle that. I already secured some space in the network. The AI this guy has are fast, but they are really dumb. Like no one ever taught them anything other than rules. I bet their code is a mess."

There was a loud whimper from the couch.

"I'll take care of the virus. I did just fine against you if I remember correctly." Ursula started the upload and used her drones to speed the process along.

"The last thing we need right now is for you two to have a pissing contest." Watching the progress, Ric sat on the desk.

"I'm going to be in so much trouble," the executive said.

Ric sighed. "Hunt, let Ursula handle the virus. You need to get your code rooted to the compute-unit. I didn't have a lot of spare cash, so there isn't much space for the two of you." A trail of warmth flowed up his arm, over his shoulder, and down to the external device in his pocket as Hunt travelled through him. The feeling was familiar and Ric realized that he had always been able to tell when Hunt moved, but it was a subtle sensation. He figured the numbness of his body helped accentuate it.

"Wow. You're not kidding. She is taking up a ton of space in here and more than half the ram. Very poorly optimized."

"Hunt, cut it out. I wouldn't have made it this far without her." Ric looked down to his shoulder where Hunt used to be housed and saw blood leaking through the flight suit. "I'm not doing so hot. My whole body is numb."

"Did they shoot one of those blue beams at you?" The executive sat up, his head peeking over the back of the couch.

"Yes." Ric furrowed his brow.

"It couldn't have hit you if you're standing. How close did it get?"

"I'm not sure. Half-a-metre?"

"Less," Ursula said.

"You'll be fine. It should wear off eventually."

"How do you know?" Ric pushed himself off the desk and paused when his feet touched the floor. He didn't feel any pain in his arms and he felt like he was floating.

"I was in charge of the project." The man lay back down.

"You designed it?"

"No." He sounded like he may cry. "I was just the project lead. I did handle the marketing though."

"That's…good." Ric felt sorry for the guy and it dampened his anger. The spineless Corporate stooge was the reason he was hurt, that Hunt was taken, and why he was stuck on a space station with security on the other side of the door—but he was so pathetic.

"Thanks. I came up with the name, too."

"Oh, yeah?"

"The Turbo-Blaster," he sniffed, "four-thousand."

Ric heard a muffled buzzing sound and smelled smoke. He glanced at the door and saw dark wisps curling away from the lock. "Shit. I guess they got tired of waiting. How's it going, you two?"

"I'm okay, I guess." The executive said. "A little sad. Maybe a bit scared, but you seem like a reasonable guy, so—"

"Not you."

He whimpered like a scolded dog.

"Hunt, Ursula?"

"I'm in the compute-unit," Hunt said. "Just freeing up some space."

Ursula said, "I got the file loaded, but it's not doing anything."

"Just hold on. I'll take care of it in a sec," Hunt said.

They sniped back and forth until Ric cut them off. "Hey. Figure it out, we're about to be raided, here." He unplugged and turned off the speaker, tuning them out in his implant as he stumbled over to the executive. "I guess you're my hostage."

"Yeah." The man wouldn't look him in the face. "Okay."

Ric took a deep breath. "So, how do I get out of here?"

"I dunno."

"Who would?"

"Maybe the Director?" Shifting, the man pulled out the pillow he'd been laying on and hugged it.

"Okay. How do I get to the Director?"

"I don't know."

"How long will it take security to break in?"

"I don't know." The executive turned his back on Ric.

"This is going nowhere." Ric felt like slumping to the ground. The only thing keeping him standing was concentration. He felt like a marionette who had to control his own strings.

I have an idea. The words appeared across Ric's projection, over top of everything else.

Ric turned the audio back on for the AI. "Which one of you typed that?"

"I did," Ursula said.

"But I have an idea, too," Hunt added.

Closing his eyes, Ric let his head drop. "Ursula first."

"We change the virus. We'll have to if we want it to infect the system anyway. With my help, and my drones, I can push it through the system faster than it could go on its own. They already know we're here, so, who cares if I set off more alarms."

Ric looked up, the possibility giving him some energy. "Huh. That's not bad. It could use tighter focus. What do you think, Hunt?"

"Uh. That's what I was going to say, but with me proliferating the virus. Right now we're boxed in with this guy's AI."

"Here's a novel idea." Ric took a step towards the desk but gave up and sat on the edge of the sofa. "Why not work together? I'll fix the virus, you two figure out a way to spread it around, taking over whatever systems you can along the way. The more control we have, the better our chances of getting off this station. In order of importance, our goals are to stop security from getting into this room, get to the Director's Office unscathed, and find a way home." He sighed and brushed back his hair. "If we can cut out the Director, all the better."

The executive sat up. "No!"

Ric nearly fell off the couch. He put a hand to his chest and felt his rapidly beating heart. "What?"

"You have to see the Director. If you can't convince her to let you go, she'll hunt you down. There is no way you'll survive with all of the Amcoral resources at her disposal."

"Why do you care?

The man looked like he would cry again. "What?"

"Why try and help me? You're the one who kidnapped my AI in the first place."

"I'm sorry. I didn't…I just…this job is hard." He squeezed the pillow tighter. "You have no idea the pressure to perform—to find the next leap forward. I was on track for a promotion to manager, but I got saddled with the AI division and," tears rolled down his face, "it was in shambles. There was no way to get an advanced AI in time for my promotion, so I had some of my contacts keep an eye open and they found you. You probably hate me."

"Yes. Very much."

Wailing, the executive buried his face in the pillow.

"But, if you help me get out of here with both my AI…" Ric made the same expression as when he drank the last shot of tequila of the night. "I'll forgive you."

"Really?"

"Hunt, Ursula, how are you doing?" Ric turned away from the blubbering man.

"Yeah, great," Hunt said. "These AI are no problem with both of us."

Ric took a deep breath to clear his head. "I wonder why the AI aren't better."

The executive peeked over the pillow. "The board doesn't really like the thought of AI. Say they aren't predictable enough. The corporation's put most of its resources behind improving algorithms instead."

"That's pretty shortsighted," Ric said.

"We need that virus," Ursula said. "It can clear a

path for us."

"Okay." Ric opened the code for the virus and brought up his virtual keyboard. His fingers were stiff and his typing clumsy, but it was easy enough to alter the code and program the worm to up its replication and infect more systems.

"You missed a bracket there." The executive had sat up again and was hovering over Ric's shoulder. He pointed to Ric's right hand.

"Thanks. Why don't you think of a way to get those guards to back off?"

"Oh, that's easy." The man sniffed. His eyes were red, but he had stopped crying.

Ric raised an eyebrow. "How?"

"You took me hostage. Demand they back off."

"And they will?"

"No. Not totally, but they'll at least make it look like they're leaving. If your AI get control of the emergency airlocks, they can create a path between here and the director's office." The corner of his lip curled up.

"That's a good plan, actually." Ric sneered. "Any suggestion on what to say to get them behind the nearest airlock?"

"Leave it to me." With a pat on Ric's back, he shot off the couch and walked to the door. When he got to the chair that Ric had pushed in front of it, he took a deep breath and winked. "Help! This man is a maniac! He said he would kill me if you didn't leave immediately. He'll do it too. He's already given me a thorough thrashing."

Ric dropped his head into his numb hands. "Who the hell is this guy?" he mumbled.

"I know, right," Hunt said.

The sound of cutting stopped, however. Perking up, Ric turned toward the door.

The executive smiled and gave him a thumbs up.

"Mister Hino? Are you alright?" someone asked through the door.

"No. I've been beaten up. Please listen to his demands." The executive, who was apparently Mister Hino, delivered his lines like he was in a community theatre play. "I'm frightened of what he will do if you don't comply."

"What are his demands?"

Hino turned to Ric and shrugged.

"Get them out of here," Ric said quietly.

Making an 'ok' with his fingers, Hino turned back to the door. "You must leave. He says if you're within two-hundred metres of this office, he will... uh. He'll—"

Ric mouthed, "Kill you."

Hino said, "Kiss me."

Despite the disconnect between his brain and his motor control, Ric managed to wave his arms in front of him. "No!"

"No! Not kiss me. But something terrible, I'm sure. Two-hundred metres, remember."

Shaking his head, Ric waved Hino over. "Is there a way for us to tell when they are far enough away? Like, is there a camera or something?"

"Not in this area. Lack of surveillance is supposed to promote competition. But maybe one of your AI friends could get into the security systems and monitor their movement." Hino tapped his head. "All their helmets are tracked."

"Hunt?"

"I'm on it."

Ric opened a window on his projection. There was a huge wall of scrolling data that the AI chewed through with ease. "Can you handle the emergency airlocks, too?"

"You bet. I'll get us a path right to the Director's office."

"What about me?" Ursula asked.

"Keep spreading that virus and get your drones into any systems you can, the more resistance, the better likelihood it's worth taking." Ric scratched his head.

The lights dimmed and there was a click. The air circulation stopped. Ric hadn't noticed the sound until it was gone. With another click, it came back on.

"That was me," Ursula said.

"Good job." With a grunt, Ric stood.

Hino rubbed his hands together. "So, what's next?"

"You're really into this."

"I love solving problems."

Ric huffed. "Next, we head to the Director's office. As soon as the way is clear."

"Any minute. I'm waiting for some stragglers to get out of the optimal route," Hunt said.

Hino clapped Ric on the shoulder hard enough to push him forward. "Well, good luck to you."

"What do you mean good luck? You're my hostage." Ric slapped him back, but had no feedback to tell how hard he hit. There was a spurt of blood that made the stain on his shoulder spread. "You're coming with me."

"Why? You have a clear path to the Director." The executive backed away.

"What if any security happened to be inside the airlocks? What if we run into that crazy secretary?"

"Who, Jeremy?"

"I don't know his name, but he chased me for a good ten minutes."

"That's Jeremy." Hino rubbed his chin. "He's a stickler for the rules."

"Then he's a perfect example. You're my hostage and you're coming with me to see the director." Ric nearly tripped and the executive caught him.

"Fine, but you're going to have to rough me up first so it doesn't look like I gave in too easily."

Ric held up his broken and bruised hand. "How am I supposed to do that?"

Hino reached out and swiped his fingers across the blood spot on Ric's flight suit and rubbed them on his face.

"That's disgusting." Ric had to look away.

"Well." Going to a white and gold-framed mirror, Hino adjusted the smears. "I'm not about to punch myself in the face."

A map of the space station appeared on Ric's projection. There was a star marking where they were in the central section and a path leading to the outer edge.

"We're set. Better hurry before someone manages to break through one of the airlocks. They're meant to keep air in, not people out," Hunt said.

"Can you two stay in the system if I leave the office?"

"You bet," Ursula said. "We can stay in the network wirelessly. The signal is really strong."

Ric took a deep breath. "Hino, ready to go?"

The executive joined him at the door. His face looked like a child had slapped him after a disturbing finger-painting session. Ric put his arm over the man's shoulder.

"I, uh. I'm not sure we're there as friends—unless this is for the hostage thing?"

Gritting his teeth, Ric shoved the chair away from the door with his foot. "It's to keep me from falling on my face until this stun wears off."

Break/Interrupt

TWENTY-NINE
Office
Politics

The hallway was clear all the way to an elevator that connected the central section to the outer ring. They travelled across one of the spokes, gravity fading in and out as they moved.

Hino had half-carried Ric down the long, carpeted corridors of the maze-like administration area. Their route had extra twists and turns due to the strategically closed emergency doors that cut off the hallways with segmented walls of steel.

As they travelled to the ring, Ric stretched his legs and twisted his back.

"What are you doing?" Hino asked.

"I'm trying to speed things along." He bent over to touch his toes, managing to reach his shins. "I'm not sure if feeling is coming back or if I'm getting used to the sensation of numbness and tingles."

"Hey, Ric?" Hunt said.

"Yeah?" As Ric straightened, two vertebrae cracked and he made a little squeak of relief.

"I thought I should let you know that the concourse on the main floor of the ring is pretty big. I managed to get the airlocks closed, but I was only able to track security guards, so there's a good chance some people got trapped inside our route."

"And why didn't you tell me this earlier?"

"Well, you showed up with a new AI and I didn't want to look bad. I hoped I would come up with a solution before now."

Inhaling, Ric held the breath and scrunched up his face. "I've been over this."

"I know, but—"

"Stop." Ric held up a finger. "It's fine. That's why we have a hostage, right?"

"Me?" Hino asked, pointing to his chest.

"Yeah, buddy." Ric put his arm around him. "This time, let's pretend I have a weapon at your side, okay?" Stuffing his left hand inside the flight suit, Ric made a finger gun and pressed it to Hino's side.

The elevator stopped and the doors opened to a cavernous space. The back wall bowed inward with windows several storeys high that were partially blocked by a balcony above them. The huge hallway, wide enough to land several Consortium ships like the one he'd come to the station on, noticeably curved up in both directions.

The view outside the windows changed as they rotated. Ric noticed the bright lights from the back end of the Goliath ship coming around the moon. The Earth slowly crept into view as the moon slipped out the other side.

Ric stepped forward and stuttered to a halt. Hino hadn't moved.

"Let's go, man." Ric smiled.

"Do we really have to? What if some of my colleagues see me?" The doors tried to close, but Hino was in the way.

"Then you have an exciting story to tell them."

"You don't understand." The executive grabbed the sleeve of Ric's flight suit. "I've stepped on a lot of people on my way up. I don't burn bridges, I steal them and submit them as my own work."

Groaning, Ric barred his clenched teeth. "Look. We both know I'm incapable of hurting you right now—I would do it if I weren't a walking corpse. What I can do is have my AI comb the network for dirty secrets and turn them over to your co-workers. Is that incentive enough?"

"Yup." Hino straightened his tie. "Let's go."

Hunt created a glowing path on the floor for Ric to follow. "Not far now. Around the bend, up an escalator, then a private staircase, and we're there."

The kidnapper and his hostage shuffled forward,

taking a few metres to fall into step with each other. Ric made sure to lift his legs to keep his feet from dragging and found it easier on the smooth floor.

The corridor unfolded in front of them as they followed the curve. They passed an escalator and Ric saw the huge metal airlock come into view. There was a dull thud and as they got closer, he saw a cluster of people standing next to the new metal wall.

"Oh, no," Hino said.

"What?" Ric pulled him closer.

"I work with them."

"All of them?" Ric counted eleven in the group and noticed a few others on their own or in pairs in the immediate area.

"Most of them."

The person knocking was a tall, broad-shouldered man in a similar suit to Hino. The stripes were in a different order and instead of wrapping around the torso, they swooped down from the lapels and met in the back at the bottom of the jacket. He filled it out better and his dark brown skin complimented the deep blue as if the colour had been designed for him.

He turned from the center of the group and opened his arms wide. "Hino. What brings you here, you barracuda? Whoa, what happened to your face?"

"Jackson! Of course I'd run into you. This is, uh, nothing." Hino smiled in the same fake way Ric did with clients and whispered into Ric's ear. "This is bad."

"What?" Ric said through his own smile.

"It's Jackson," Hino hissed as if that would answer the question. "Abort."

"I'm not aborting anything." They kept walking steadily forward and were standing in front of the group before Ric realized he'd passed Hunt's marked path.

Jackson took a deep breath and smirked. Reaching behind him, his jacket straining against his muscles, he knocked on the barrier. "What do you make of this, Hino? Not one of your experiments gone wrong, I hope?"

The group laughed.

"Not me." Hino was stiff, but Ric could feel him trembling. "I was saddled with AI, remember?"

"That's right." Jackson took a step and the others parted for him. "A test to see if you're worthy of promotion, if I'm not mistaken. Who's your friend here?"

"This—um." Hino coughed. "Yes."

Reaching out to Ric, Jackson grabbed the patch on his chest in his thumb and forefinger. "Larry? How do you know Hino?"

"We had a meeting and, uh…" Hino shrugged.

Jackson let go of Ric's flight suit and smoothed it down. "You look like shit, Larry." He turned to

Hino. "Your friend is bleeding. What have you gotten yourself into?"

"That?" Hino chuckled nervously. "We ran into a little trouble, I should get him some medical attention."

"You know." Jackson stuffed his hands into his pockets. "There was a security guard here a minute ago. He said something about a hostage, in our area no less. That wouldn't be the trouble you mean?"

Hino ran, pulling Ric along with him. "Go!"

Ric struggled to get his feet under him. He dug his heels in, slowing Hino enough to turn him towards the escalator. "What's going on?"

"He's onto us. Why didn't you pull your kidnapper routine?"

"You started talking to the guy, I just went with it." Ric abandoned the fake gun idea and grabbed the railing to the escalator, swinging them up the first step. The power was off making them just stairs. "Who is that guy?"

The escalator was wide enough for them to scramble up side-by-side. Hino seemed to have forgotten that Ric had his arm around him for stability and charged ahead. "He's my rival. At least, I see him as a rival. He kind of leads the floor, as you could see."

Ric peered over the side and saw the big man chasing after them, the group of office workers in his wake. "Well, he's after us."

They were near the top when Jackson grabbed onto the arm Ric had on Hino's shoulders. With a quick tug, Ric was dangling over the side of the railing, his tingling legs kicking out to find purchase.

"Who are you?" Jackson said calmly, in total control. "What is Hino up to this time?"

Ric sneered. With Jackson grabbing him around the wrist, his shattered hand throbbed. He felt like a child—helpless. Looking past the broad shoulders, he saw Hino pinned down by the other executives.

"Answer me or security will be talking to you when you wake up from the coma." Smiling, Jackson let Ric drop a hand length. He swung in the man's grip, his knees bashing into the side of the escalator.

"I've gone through too much to let you stop me." Ric Forced himself to smile back. "I was cut open by the likes of you and my friend was taken from me. I survived and managed to get aboard your station, got him back, and now I'm going to find a way home." With his free hand, Ric typed out a message. *I'm screwed here. Any ideas?*

"What friend? That shit, Hino?"

Ric shook his head.

"I'll give you a way off the station. It'll be out the airlock with the rest of the trash." Jackson's smile broke as he let go.

On his way down, Ric felt the uneven pull of the

artificial gravity. The floor drifted as he fell towards it.

The concourse went dark. Red lights flashed as a siren wailed and the nearby emergency airlock started to rise. Colliding with the ground, Ric thought the impact wasn't nearly as bad as he expected. The wind was knocked out of him, but the station's rotation slowed and he floated back towards the escalator.

He heaved. "What happened?"

"I cut the gravity," Ursula said. "But that reset all the airlocks that Hunt closed. Sorry."

"Better than breaking my neck." Ric saw Hino and some of Jackson's groupies fly towards the ceiling, thrown from the escalator as the rotation ground to a stop. Most of the executives seemed preoccupied with their own weightlessness. Only two of them were still hanging on to Hino, causing them to spin like a malformed model of a molecule. Ric was sure there was screaming, but the siren muffled the sound.

Jackson hung on to the railing, his feet still planted on the step. As Ric got closer, the man reached for him. "Get back here so I can deal with you properly," he screamed.

"No thanks." Ric tried to swim away, managing to get himself to spin.

Grabbing him by the scruff of his borrowed

flight suit, Jackson reeled him in. Ric fumbled with the zipper, feeling creeping back into his extremities. Using the aggressive pull, he slipped out of the suit and was launched towards the ceiling.

He crashed into three executives clinging to each other and ended up with one of them hanging on to his leg. Not sure if the woman held on for fear or in an attempt to catch him, Ric kicked her off, throwing himself off balance when he hit the ceiling and sending him ricocheting towards the windows.

"What was that?" Hunt asked.

"I was trying to kick off the ceiling, but that woman got in the way." Ric crossed his arms in front of him and collided with the curved window, sending him back to the floor. Groaning, he grabbed his bleeding shoulder and saw the streak he'd left along the glass. Beyond it, he noticed the view of the Earth was hardly moving.

"You're definitely leaving DNA," Ursula added.

Ric was close enough to the wall to use it to slow down and land on the floor feet first. He still bounced off of it, but he wasn't in an uncontrolled drift towards Jackson again. "I'm trying, here. It's harder than it looks and I'm injured."

Both AI yelled on top of each other. "Heads up!"

Looking back towards the top of the escalator, Ric expected to see the executive barreling towards him, but the man wasn't there. Someone screamed over the siren, drawing his attention to where the airlock had been. A squad of armored security guards floated towards him, some more towards than others. Ric didn't have time to count. He was just above the floor and heading under the balcony with no way to change his direction.

"That's six guards," Hunt said. "Two are on a close trajectory."

"The others can shoot you," Ursula added.

"Great." Ric arched his back when he reached the wall. Tucking in his legs, he launched himself at the outside edge of the balcony. Speeding towards the lip, he tried to hold on, but didn't have a good enough grip. Gritting his teeth, he planned for another bounce off the windows, but he jerked to a stop.

Jackson had made his way along the railings and managed to catch him by the ankle. He said something, but Ric couldn't hear over the siren.

Ric tried to kick him, but the big man easily deflected the attacks. Twisting and flailing, he tried to break free. His foot clipped the railing and he pushed against it, forcing Jackson to grab him with both hands. In his desperate thrashing, Ric saw that Jackson had his feet hooked under the bottom bar of the railing.

Using the leverage from Jackson's vice-grip, Ric

bent and unhooked the executive's feet. Before Jackson could react, Ric flipped him over the railing and sent him careening into the blood smear he'd left on the windows.

Hunt said, "Good Job."

"Yeah," Ursula added.

They both told him to get moving.

Clinging to the railing, Ric used it like a track to traverse the balcony, following the path that was still marked on his projection.

Looking behind him, Ric saw the chaos he was leaving. Hino had been grabbed by one of the guards, though the people who had tumbled away with him were clinging to the guard's legs and the group was drifting away. A few other guards were as lost as the executives, bouncing or floating with no control. Two of them seemed to still be following him, but it was hard to tell in the commotion and flashing lights.

Jackson was definitely making his way towards him, expertly bounding away from the ceiling and diving to the railing.

Ric felt the metal vibrate as Jackson grabbed hold of it and started his chase. With the feeling coming back, Ric ground his teeth through the pain in his hand—though his shoulder overwhelmed everything else. Each tug on the railing pulled the plate farther free and opened the stitches a little more. He took larger swings to gain speed, risking losing hold of the railing, but every time he glanced back, Jackson was closer.

The man seemed to be foaming at the mouth. Pulsing veins stood out on his unblemished forehead.

Changing his angle, Ric got on the inside of the railing, facing the windows through it. Rather than just pull with his hands, he kicked off of the posts like a dog climbing a ladder. He was going faster and knew that Jackson would probably follow his example, but he hoped he could keep far enough ahead to make the leap to the quickly approaching stairwell.

"You see it, right?" Ursula asked.

Hunt said, "I got the door."

Ric didn't answer. Letting his feet get ahead of his hands, he stood upright on one of the posts and jumped. Momentum kept him careening forward as he reached for the stairwell. He hit the wall early and spun, but enough of him made it into the doorway for him to stop. The door slid closed and he managed to get inside before the safety mechanism forced it back open again.

He heard a slam as Jackson hit the door. With nothing to grab onto, Ric figured he must have ricocheted away.

"What now?" Ursula asked. "Want me to get the

gravity going again?"

"Is it out in the whole station?" Ric lay still. The numbness mostly gone, he hurt everywhere. He was able to make a fist with both hands, though.

"Yeah. It's all or nothing."

"Can you do it slowly, so people won't smash into the floor?"

"That's how it works anyway."

Ric felt a lurch, like a car stalling. The floor moved towards him as the station began to turn. "Hunt?"

"Yeah?"

"Is this door solid? Like, am I on a time limit or will it keep security out?"

"It's the most secure door on the station outside of the engine and life support sections. I can keep it locked down, but they'll eventually cut through it."

"How long?" Ric felt the pull on his body. His legs were lying up the stairs and his head was on the landing. He spoke slowly, not wanting to aggravate any of his wounds.

"I'm not an expert. I don't even know what kind of equipment they have. Best guess would be half-an-hour if they used the same stuff that they did on the office door."

Sighing, Ric rolled onto his side and got himself seated. "I assume they'll be more aggressive if they think their Director is in danger."

"That's fair."

"Makes sense to me, if anyone was interested," Ursula said.

Ric groaned. "I guess it's time to go to work."

THIRTY
Bidding War

On his way up the stairs, Ric called Lien, hoping she hadn't given him a fake number. There was a long pause before it rang. As it did, he got to the reception area at the top of the stairs like a mountain climber reaching the summit. Breathing heavily, his legs dragging, he almost felt a high from the exhaustion.

There was a skinny, stiff-looking guy behind a standing desk and office supplies scattered around the room. He wore an orange bowtie and a crisp blue shirt. When he turned to see who was coming up the stairs, his bangs followed a moment later in a single, congealed clump. He jerked away from Ric.

"Who are you?"

Ric sighed. "I sneaked onto the station because one of your executives kidnapped a friend of mine. I'm here to see the Director about a way home."

"You remind me of someone." The assistant

crossed his arms.

Smirking, Ric brushed back his hair. "That's funny. I could say the same for you."

The call to Lien connected and video of the Consortium agent popped up on Ric's projection. "What do you want? I'm not going to get you out of whatever trouble you're in."

The assistant reached under his desk and Ric figured he was signaling for help. "I can't allow you to see the Director. Have a seat. Security will be here any second."

"No they won't." Ric took a step towards a set of big wooden doors. "I'm going to see if the Director is willing to trade for control over her space station."

"I can't let you do that." The man came out from behind his desk.

Lien looked off to the side and waved for someone to come over to her. "Ric. Did you manage to get control over the station? I can't see what's going on. Patch me into a camera."

Hunt said, "Want me to do that?"

Ric nodded.

"So, you agree with me?" The assistant smiled like a child who tattled and got another kid in trouble. "Have a seat." He gestured to a chair sitting crookedly next to a side table.

There was a machine on it Ric didn't recognize.

It lay on its side and looked a little like a drink dispenser, but much bulkier and it had a rough finish. Ric picked it up and the secretary flinched. "This something important?"

"Put that down!"

Lien laughed. "This is the dorkiest stand-off I've ever seen."

Ric faked tossing the device making the secretary jerk forward, ready to lunge. "Look, man. You can see how beat up I am. Your people's fault by the way. I managed to get onto your station and all the way here. I'm not going to let you stop me even if you're a secret ninja or have crazy cyborg parts. I won't hurt your Director. I just want a way home."

"And I told you to have a seat." The thin man dove at him.

Jumping back, Ric nearly fell down the stairs. He hit his shin on the top step, but the secretary landed in front of him. With a grunt, he swung the device down at the man's head.

The assistant covered up with his arms, but the object was heavy and some of the force made it through. He wailed in pain.

With a last burst of energy, Ric leaped over the downed man. He landed on the side of his foot and sprained his ankle. Swearing, he limped the rest of the way to the Director's office bursting through the doors.

"Hey. I'm—"

"I know who you are." A tall woman in a blue and white dress that cut down sharply from the shoulders was leaning on an antique looking wood desk that would have taken up most of Ric's apartment. The rest of the huge office was similarly decorated but looked like someone had tossed the place, Ric figured because the gravity had cut out. Everything was dark wood or leather. Old books were tipped over on shelves or scatted across the floor. A standing globe managed to stay upright in the corner.

The woman took a big step forward and Ric noticed one of her shoes was white and the other was orange. She went to a couch in the middle of the room and gestured for him to sit in an identical one that mostly faced it.

Ric limped towards her but stopped short next to a coffee table in-between the sofas. "I'm fine here."

"Really?" She laughed. "You don't look fine. You're bleeding all down your shirt."

"This shouldn't take long." Ric could feel the blood soaking into fabric, already damp from his sweat.

The assistant came stumbling into the room holding the back of his head.

"Stop," the Director said. "Go, and close the door behind you."

"Ma'am?" The man looked from her to Ric and back.

"I'll handle this, since it seems no one else has been able to."

The assistant bowed and Ric could see the hair on the back of his head was plastered down with blood. Feeling his cheeks flush, he looked away as the door closed.

The woman leaned back and crossed her legs. "Do you know who I am?"

Ric almost laughed. "The Director."

"My name is Victoria."

"Oh, are we exchanging names now, because you cut me off a second ago."

Smiling, Victoria tilted her head to the side. "I have a good idea of your name. Ulrich, right?"

"Is that supposed to throw me off guard? That one of the thousand people here was able to look me up?" He sniffed.

"I know your brother."

The woman hadn't blinked since had she sat. Ric was too aware of his own eyelids and felt like he was blinking too much. "My brother works for Telbak."

"He used to. Now he works for me." Finally closing her eyes, she took a moment before opening them again. "And I think you could, too. Even though you made a mess of my office."

"If you kill her right now," Lien said, "I will

guarantee you a way home."

"No." Ric clenched his teeth.

"But you haven't even heard my offer," Victoria said.

"I don't need to. All I need is a way back to Earth. In exchange, you get your station back."

"And the virus?" The director waved her hand over the table and an image of the worm and Ursula's drone attack in the network appeared in the space above it.

"Yeah, Ric?" Lien asked. "What about the virus?"

"Once I leave and my AI stop pushing it through the system, your people should be able to take care of it." The peripheral of Ric's vision dimmed and he swayed on his feet.

"But if you worked for me, you could do it. And so many other things. You could work with your brother again."

"I don't give a shit about my brother." Ric sneered. "All he ever wanted was to leave. Leave the city. Leave the planet. He left Telbak and came here. I'd be surprised if he wasn't about to leave you too."

Victoria stopped smiling. Her face was so still she looked like a picture of a person. A 3D representation made for virtual reality. "I can't let you just go. You've caused too much trouble. If you worked for me, I could spare your life. Maybe you'll find a place here, brother or not."

Ric brushed back his hair. Looking out the window that took up the entire back wall, he saw evidence of the enhanced virus throughout the station. The empty blackness between the ring and the core was constantly being interrupted by flashes of light and miscellaneous debris spilling out of venting airlocks. "Your space station isn't in very good shape. Like me." He met her stoic gaze. "It's beat up. Tired. And instead of having the time to heal, I'm here. Making things worse for both of us."

"What do you want?"

"I want to go home. I came here because your people took my friend from me. Cut him out of my body." Ric touched the growing red spot on his shoulder. "What I really want is for this to be over, but I doubt that's possible."

The Director leaned forward. "No. Like I said, my position dictates that I can't just forget what you've done, even if my people were the aggressors. It's a blemish on the otherwise pristine system of Corporatocrasy."

"That doesn't leave me with a lot of options." Ric watched the image of the network floating over the table.

"I'm afraid not. Personally, as the private individual, Victoria, I am sorry for what happened to you. I don't ask questions when it comes to new acquisitions because I started in the same job and I know what goes on. Not that I would do anything to stop it. That wouldn't stop our competitors and we can't give them that kind of advantage."

"I don't care." Ric shook his head. "That's too big. What matters right now is finding a resolution."

"Very well. What do you propose?"

"You shot down my proposition. It's your turn?"

"Give up." She stood. "If you won't work for me then turn the AI over to our research and development department."

Ric walked away. He had to move to keep alert. "You may as well ask me to give up a child. I went through all this to get him back."

"And the other one."

Shaking his head, Ric headed towards the window. "I promised."

"Ric," Hunt said. "They're making an organized push to get back control of the network."

With his back to the Director, Ric typed on his thigh. *Can you stop it?*

"Not for long," Ursula said.

"And not without causing some damage, maybe hurting some people," Hunt added.

Ric was next to the desk. He leaned against it in nearly the same position the Director had been when he walked in. "You're trying to take the station back."

"We will. Like you said, it's only a matter of

time." Victoria went over to the globe, lifted the top, and poured herself a glass from one of the bottles inside. She held the drink up to him.

He shook his head. "You're backing me into a corner. You won't let me leave and you're trying to take my only bargaining chip. That's enough to make a person do something desperate."

Lien said, "I sent the ship back. It will be there soon to pick you up, but I won't give the order unless you make it worth my while."

"What do you want?" Ric asked.

"If you won't kill her. Cripple the station. Steal information. Cause as much damage as you can. If you do well enough, I'll signal the ship to get you."

Victoria drained her glass and slammed it down hard enough to crack it. "I'm done playing games with you. The offer of a job is gone. It's the AI—both of them, or I kill you myself."

"Sounds like you may have to kill her after all." Lien chuckled.

"Did you hear that?" Ric asked.

Lien and Victoria replied but Ric wasn't listening to them.

"I was built for this," Ursula said. "Just give me the word."

"The people?" Hunt asked.

"Do your best." Ric took a deep breath and strode to the display of the network.

"I'm not just a pencil pusher." Victoria took her shoes off. "I've gotten my hands plenty dirty and you at your best wouldn't be a challenge."

Ric sneered at her. "I'm not talking to you." He nodded to the representation of the network. Whole sections were going black. The station shuddered as loud sounds of grinding, crashing, and explosions made their way to the office. "This is your last chance. A way home, now, or I take the other offer on the table."

"What other offer?" Victoria's expression sank. "You have someone else listening in. That shouldn't be possible. It would be detected."

"Your network is in shambles. One of your executives installed my AI into your system and right around your firewalls. Not very smart. They can cause a lot of damage before you stop them."

There was a huge flash behind them. They turned to see a plume of fire escape the core section before the air was used up and the vacuum put it out.

The sleek, black Consortium ship flew right next to the window making them both flinch.

Victoria cut off a yelp and turned the sound into a growl. "You're working for the Consortium?"

"Your people forced my hand. The Consortium offered me a ride here." Ric typed a message, hoping the action would go unnoticed in the chaos. *We're leaving, now!*

He felt the AI travel through his implant. They both sent an acknowledgement that they were back. "Is that good enough?" he asked.

Lien didn't answer, but the ship turned its rear hatch to the window.

Ric blinked. His peripheral vision was patchy, but he was sure that he saw the ship properly.

"How are we supposed to get on it?" Hunt said, voicing the same concern Ric had.

"Fine," Victoria said. "The job offer is back on the table. Stop what you're doing to the station and I'll forgive everything."

"I don't want anything to do with you."

"I'm a better option than they are." The Director waved a hand at the ship. "They are nothing but a flea on our underbelly. We can offer you so much more."

Ric let his mouth fall open. "I'm not joining them. I used to think that Corporations were a necessary evil. Now, I think you're all a blight. Holding us back."

Lien cleared her throat. "If you accept the ride, you work for us. That's non-negotiable."

Laughing, Ric brushed back his hair. "Fine—better than here. How do I get on the ship?"

The hatch opened and the ship backed into the window making a deep thud. From around the opening, an umbilical shot out, sealing against the glass.

Sparks blasted from inside the ring, cutting through the resilient material.

"Well, hurry up," Ric said seeing the slow progress.

Victoria lunged at him with a kick. Her foot hit his shoulder, sending him into the coffee table.

Ric held the wound as blood flowed freely from it. He was sure the stitches were all split and the panel was loose.

"Look out!" Ursula said.

Screaming through his teeth he rolled off the table.

Her heel smashed down and the projection vanished.

Breathing rapidly, Ric felt alternating waves of nausea and fatigue assail him. He was on the verge of blacking out. Shuffling on his knees, he crawled towards the desk. Glancing at the window, he saw that the opening was less than half way cut.

Something flew at him and he dropped onto his stomach. The shock made him throw up in his mouth. Glass and alcohol rained on him and he realized that Victoria had thrown one of her bottles from the globe.

"I'll kill you before you get a chance to leave." She ran for him and leaped onto the desk.

As he pushed himself up, Ric felt a shard of glass next to him. Grabbing it, he stood and stabbed the Director's bare foot.

She screamed and pulled the glass free, but as she bent over, Ric grabbed her hair and let his knees give out, dragging her to the floor.

He pulled himself away with his bruised hand. He wasn't sure if the bones were healed, but he couldn't feel it and escape was more important. As he slid to the other side of the desk, he felt a sharp pain in his calf. Screaming again, he saw the same piece of glass that he'd stabbed the Director with sticking out of his leg.

Victoria looked dazed. She was sitting up but her head moved erratically, like she couldn't keep it still. She stood, the broken pieces of bottle crunching under her feet.

Ric pulled the glass free. His hand was sliced open and nearly as much blood flowed from his calf as his shoulder. He felt as weak and as disoriented as the Director looked. For a moment, he wondered why the assistant hadn't intervened, but he figured the Director's orders were not to be disobeyed.

She glowered down at him, walking around the desk on unsteady legs. She left a trail of bloody footprints and stopped next to the huge window. "Nice try." She smiled, her teeth red.

Ric closed his eyes, ready for her to pounce. He was sure she would land the killing blow and he was too weak to stop it.

Break/Interrupt

There was a loud thump.

When he looked, he saw the director in a crumpled heap on the floor. Wiping his face with his wrist, he looked again and noticed the thick disc of the window on top of her.

A man dressed in black armor, his face covered in an opaque mask, dropped into the office. "Holy crap. You're a mess."

Ric recognized the voice of the pilot, but he couldn't respond.

"Well, come on." The man picked him up and dragged him into the ship, leaving a trail of blood. "I was ordered to bring you back, but I'm no medic. I don't even know how you're still alive right now."

Ric didn't have time to wonder before he passed out.

THIRTY-ONE
Consortium Agent

Ric woke up in a room he didn't recognize. It was bare with a dull metal ceiling and walls. There was a drape covering most of his view. He tried to connect to his network, then any network.

"Hunt? Ursula?"

The AI didn't respond. He patted the bed around him and checked the small rolling table at his side, but didn't see any sign of the external compute-unit. Panicking, he threw the covers back, got out of bed, and fell.

A woman in black scrubs with red stripes down the side plodded over to him. "You're awake, finally. And too stupid to stay in bed, I see." She pulled the curtain back. "Call Agent Lien."

With the curtain retracted, Ric could see he was in a tiny hospital room with three other beds. The ceiling was low and curved inward at the corners. A similarly dressed man left the room and the nurse helped him back into bed.

"What happened? Where am I?" Ric asked.

The nurse pursed her lips. "Not my pay grade." As soon as Ric was back in bed, she headed for the door. "You'll be okay, if you rest."

Almost as soon as she left, Lien came in. "I didn't believe it. You're awake."

Ric clenched his teeth. "Where am I? Where are Hunt and Ursula?"

Lien laughed. "Typical." She hopped up and sat on the end of his bed. "We're in a secret Consortium base. Your AI, and mine, by the way, are already working. It took me a while to convince them, but once you were out of the worst of it, I told them the best way they could help you was to make sure this place was safe."

"What happened?" Ric squeezed his fists and stretched out his arms. "I mean, I thought I was going to die and I feel pretty good, considering."

"It's the strangest thing." Lien patted his leg over the covers. "You were a mess when you got here. Blood everywhere. I thought you were a goner for sure. It turns out those AI of yours managed to take control of the nanites in your blood and used them to keep you alive. It was just enough for our medical staff to handle the rest."

Ric touched his shoulder and felt a scar through

his gown.

"I made sure you got a new compute-unit. State of the art." She brought her legs up and laid them next to him. "With enough room for Hunt and," she cleared her throat, "Ursula. I feel like I should be mad about that one."

Shrugging, Ric scrunched his nose. "She chose the name."

Lien chuckled. "That's not what I mean."

"So." Ric shifted to sit more upright. "How long have I—"

"Couple weeks. We had to pump you with a ton of nanites to speed things along. All added to your debt to the Consortium."

"And where is this place?" Ric looked around.

"We're in the Wall."

Ric nearly jumped out of bed again. "The Wall?"

"Yeah. It's a great place to hide. We're underground, but not too far. It gets really weird and dangerous the deeper you go."

Settling, Ric covered a yawn. "So, what now?"

"Now that you're up, I'll tell Hunt and Ursula. I'm sure they'll want to get settled in that compute-unit of yours. In a few days, when you're fully healed, I'll put you to work. I'm sure Amcoral got enough data on Hunt and Ursula to cause us some trouble." Lien got to her feet. "But you're a Consortium agent now." She smiled. "I was promoted because of you, so I get to be your boss."

Ric felt an intense headache that subsided as quickly as it hit.

"Ric!" Hunt said through his implant. "You're okay!"

"I was worried too," Ursula added.

Lien patted his leg again. "I see your friends found out. I'll let you get settled. You've got a lot of work ahead of you. All three of you."

COMING SOON

SNOW FROM

A

DISTANT SKY

Acknowledgements

This novella was written during the pandemic of 2020/21. It was a strange and difficult time for everyone. Though, even with their lives upended, I had no trouble finding people eager to lend me a hand. Unfortunately, I wasn't able to get my parents an early copy and I missed their critiques and comments. They continue to be my biggest supporters and I doubt I could ever pay them back. Though, I'm sure they wouldn't want me to. I hope they like the book and the surprise makes it even better.

If you've read any of the acknowledgement pages in my other books, you can probably guess that the first person to read the novella was Christian Laforet. Having someone I can trust to take the time to read my stuff when it's as its most rough is invaluable. He can always be counted on to be critical and keep it constructive. I'm only a little sorry I made him read a draft that was so much longer than the final cut.

My brother was a constant encouragement through this one. He was so excited to read it that he made me that much more eager to get it finished (and make sure it was good). Hearing him hard at work on his music was a helpful reminder that I should keep working, too.

One of the best resources I've found is the Writing Wrecking Crew. The small group of mostly like-minded writers have helped kept me sane through this long year. Even if its just a message to the group asking who else is writing that morning or an opinion on something that's keeping the next chapter from being finished. They are all amazing, supportive, and they keep me on my toes.

Brittni Brinn, Justin Cantello, Sephorah Pohjola, Melissa Schnarr-Rice, James Martin, and Michael Drakich in particular, gave me edits along the way. They caught so many mistakes and gave me incredible suggestions. No book is written alone and this one is held up by their creativity and hard work. I've come to rely on those people and hope I have been half as helpful when they've called on me.

I. Sylvano is a personal favourite author of mine. I've had the privilege to see him work and he's fast enough to be intimidating. He creates amazing worlds and I'm thankful that he gave me such a great quote for the back of this book.

Glen Hawkes outdid himself with the cover. He impressed me with the cover to Broadcast Wasteland, but this time he came up with more of the design, rather than make what I had come up with work, and it shows. Not only is he singularly talented, he's also a joy to work with.

Ben Van Dongen was born in Windsor Ontario. He likes to think that if he tried harder he could have been an Astronaut, but he is happier writing science fiction anyway. He wrote the Synthetic Albatross Novella Series, co-authored the books No Light Tomorrow and All These Crooked Streets, and is one half of the founding team of Adventure Worlds Press. You can read more crazy notions on his website. **BenVanDongen.com**

Photo by Khoa Nguyen

AdventureWorldsPress.com

More Books by the Author

The Synthetic Albatross Series

The Earth Books
The Thinking Machine
The Neon Heart
Break/Interrupt

The Offworld Books
Broadcast Wasteland

Anthologies
No Light Tomorrow
All These Crooked Streets

.